DANNY ORLIS
AND
ROBIN'S REBELLION

DANNY ORLIS
AND
ROBIN'S REBELLION

BERNARD PALMER

Danny Orlis and Robin's Rebellion
© 2024 by Bernard Palmer
All rights reserved. First edition 1966.
Second edition 2024.

Cover image: Adobe Firefly

Character illustrations: John Ball

Editor: Jon D. Fogdall

Aneko Press Youth

www.anekopress.com

Aneko Press, Life Sentence Publishing, and our logos are trademarks of Life Sentence Publishing, Inc.
203 E. Birch Street
P.O. Box 652
Abbotsford, WI 54405

JUVENILE FICTION / Religious / Christian / Action & Adventure

Paperback ISBN: 979-8-88936-030-8

eBook ISBN: 979-8-88936-031-5

10 9 8 7 6 5 4 3 2 1

Available where books are sold

CONTENTS

FIRST ENCOUNTER

Football season had come to Fairview, Minnesota. Around the high school nobody noticed the brilliant hues of the autumn leaves or the frosty chill of the mornings. Fairview High had a winning team, and the guys who were fortunate enough to be in the starting lineup suddenly became very special individuals. The other boys looked up to them, and the girls all but swooned should one of the new elite so much as glance their way.

Linda Penner was as excited about the football season as anyone at school. She didn't miss a game if she could help it and was usually in the front row of the cheering section. She may have been as interested in the members of the team as most of the rest of her girlfriends, but she didn't show it. She didn't go out of her way to talk with them or make any attempt to attract their attention.

One afternoon she stayed to talk with one of her teachers about an assignment for the next day and was slow getting to her locker. She was putting on her coat when Alex Smith came up. He was tall and broad shouldered with a shock of blond hair and eyes that laughed merrily when he talked. Alex was not only *on* the football team. He was the new star.

"Hi," he said, stopping beside her.

Linda looked up at him. Her smile was friendly. "Hi, Alex."

"All ready for that history test in the morning?"

Linda shuddered. "I don't believe I'll ever be ready for a history test. It gives me goose bumps just to think about it."

He laughed easily. "Oh, come on now. It's not as bad as all that."

"Maybe it isn't, but you'll never convince me of that. History is one of those subjects I can do without."

"History's always been a favorite subject of mine." He paused momentarily. "If you ever need any help with history, just whistle and I'll come running."

"Thanks, but I've been able to manage OK so far."

He seemed disappointed. "You never know when you'll need a little help."

Her smile flashed again. "If I do, I'll know who to call on."

She picked up her books and would have gone out of the building had Alex not stopped her.

"Just a minute, Linda." He caught up with her.

"There's a great show at the theater beginning tomorrow night. If you're not already booked up, I sure would like to have you go with me." There was a certain confidence in his voice that revealed his own belief that she would be very pleased to go with him. Linda, however, had a different idea.

"Thank you, Alex," she told him frankly, "but I don't go to movies."

Curiosity glinted in his eyes. "Don't go to movies?" he echoed. "Now that's a switch. What's the trouble? Are you allergic to them?"

She laughed pleasantly. "I'm a Christian," she explained, "and I feel that it's better for me not to go to places like that."

He frowned. "I never heard of anything so stupid. I suppose you don't dance either."

"I used to, but I don't anymore."

Alex shook his head in disbelief. "I'm a Christian too, but I sure don't let it bother my having a good time." He laughed sarcastically. "I have my fun."

Linda chose to ignore the tone of his voice. "So do I. In fact, our whole gang has a lot of fun. Only there are things that we feel it's best for us not to do."

Alex would not let the subject drop.

"If you don't go to shows and won't dance, I suppose we could do something else." He thought a moment then asked, "How about it?"

Briefly she considered his suggestion.

"I'm sorry, Alex," she said as gently as possible,

"but I'm afraid I won't be able to go with you even though we don't go to the show or a dance. Thanks just the same."

For an instant, questions gleamed in his eyes. Then slowly they turned to anger.

"I don't know who you think you are that you're too good to go with a guy!" he exploded. "But suit yourself. I can assure you that you won't get another chance to do it."

With that he turned on his heel and stormed away.

Linda watched him momentarily, an amused look on her face. She still had not moved when a friend came hurrying over to her.

"You were talking to Alex Smith!" she exclaimed. Awe filled her voice.

Linda nodded.

"I've been dying to get to talk to him. Tell me, how did you get him to stop and talk to you?"

"I didn't. He just came up and wanted a date."

The other girl gasped.

"A date with Alex Smith? You're kidding!"

"It's the truth."

"Lucky you!" She lowered her voice. "Where are you going?"

"Oh, I'm not going with him," Linda said indifferently.

Her friend stared at her in disbelief.

"Not going with him?" she echoed. "Are you out of your ever-loving mind?"

* * *

The activities of the church Danny and Kay Orlis attended in Fairview had been somewhat curtailed during the summer months with the vacation of the pastor and so many of the congregation. However, with the coming of fall and the chill of impending winter, the calendar began to fill.

Bill Riley, one of the young men of the congregation who had gone out to Indonesia as a missionary, was home on his first furlough and was scheduled to speak at the fall missionary rally. As soon as Tom Channing heard that Bill would be back and was going to appear in their church, he asked his mother if they could have the young missionary stay with them.

"Well–." She spoke reluctantly. "I haven't finished the fall house cleaning yet."

"That won't make any difference, Mom," Tom assured her. "He probably won't even know the difference. Can't we have him?"

"If it means so much to you, I suppose it would be all right."

"That's great, Mom. Thanks." Impulsively Tom stooped and kissed her on the cheek. "He's one guy I've sure been wanting to talk to." There was a short pause. "He and I have a lot in common."

Their eyes met.

"What do you mean, Tom?" Fear etched itself in her voice.

"He's from our church," he explained, "and he's the last guy to go into full-time Christian service."

There was a short silence.

"I don't see what that has to do with you."

"Nothing, I guess," he replied lamely. "Only, it looks as though I'm going to be our next missionary."

The hurt leaped to her eyes, but she tried to hide it.

"Then too," Tom went on, "he's working in Indonesia. And for some reason, the Lord has really been impressing me with that place the last few weeks."

"You–you mean you're thinking about going out there" his mother asked, "as a–a missionary?"

"I don't know for sure about that. I guess I've just got to wait for the Lord to lead, but I feel as though I've got to talk with Bill."

Mrs. Channing managed a nervous little laugh.

"Tom, it gives me the chills to hear you talk that way."

"Now, Mom," he said, putting his arm about her shoulders with tender affection, "you know it's a real privilege to serve the Lord."

"But you'll be so far away from–from us."

"We'll still be close together – in heart."

"I know." She smiled up at him through misty eyes. "But it's so hard to see you go and to know that it will be years before we'll be able to see you again."

He did not answer her immediately.

* * *

The last of the week Tom had another date with Robin Evans to take her to young people's meeting. That evening all she could talk about was the coming missionary rally.

"I'm so excited about it, Tom, that I can hardly wait." Robin's eyes sparkled. "Just think. Bill used to belong to our young people's society. He was like one of us. And then God called him to the mission field. Now he's home on furlough."

"Did I tell you? He's going to be staying at our house."

"How wonderful. I hope I'll get a chance to talk with him."

"You will." There was a short silence. "All you have to do is come over to the house. He'll be glad to talk to you, I know."

They crossed the street and turned toward the place where Tom had parked the family car.

"You know, Tom," Robin went on, "whenever I think about someone like Bill Riley and see what he's doing for the Lord, I'm confident down deep in my heart that God wants me to be a missionary too."

Tom drove downtown, wheeled around the corner, and pulled up to the curb near the drugstore.

"How about going in for some ice cream or something cold to drink?" he asked her.

"That sounds like a great idea."

Together they went into the drugstore. A dozen or so high school kids were loitering in the place as Tom and Robin pushed their way back to a booth and ordered. Before the waitress came with their soft drinks, Alex Smith came walking up the aisle.

"Hi, Tom," he said. His smile was friendly.

"Hi, Alex."

The footballer stopped for a moment.

"Good practice we had this afternoon, wasn't it?"

"It sure was." And then Tom remembered that he hadn't introduced Robin to Alex. "Have you ever met Robin Evans?"

"I don't think I have, but this is a pleasant surprise." He looked her over appraisingly. "I've seen you around school, haven't I?"

"I–I suppose so," she stammered. "I've seen you in the halls from time to time. And of course, I've seen you on the football field."

"Everybody has seen me on the football field," he reminded her.

For some reason, her face flushed and the quiet, easy manner she had around most boys fled. She was strangely flustered.

Alex sat down beside Tom briefly and talked with him and Robin about the football team, about Fairview, and about school in general. Robin did not say much until there was a lull in the conversation.

"How do you like it here in Fairview?" she asked.

"I missed Minot at first," he said, flashing her a quick smile, "but I'm beginning to like Fairview. In fact, the more people I meet the better I like it."

Robin flushed a deep scarlet.

Tom turned the subject back to football.

"We're sure glad to have you here," he said. "I think we're going to be able to win the championship now that we've got you in our backfield."

Alex spoke carelessly. "Minot was conference champion last year," he told them. "Some of the people said it was because I played with them."

"That's the way they're talking around here. Some of the guys say that we've got it made if you don't get hurt and if we get any kind of breaks during the games."

Alex told them about several games at Minot in which he had starred the previous year. At last he looked at his watch.

"Oh, oh. I've got to get going. Training, you know. It was nice meeting you, Robin. I'll see you around."

While he was leaving the store, her gaze followed him to the door.

"Well," Tom asked, "what do you think of him?"

"Is he always so–so conceited?"

"Not on the football field. He's a great guy. The guys all think he's tops."

She picked up her spoon thoughtfully.

"He is sort of cute at that."

* * *

Fairview won the next football game handily.

Tom was fast enough to stay out in front of Alex and heavy enough to open holes for him. With Tom in the backfield, the coach was able to use the newcomer to much better advantage. With the protection Tom helped to provide, Alex ran, passed, and punted with ease. And if the opposition ganged up on Alex, the quarterback could call for Tom to carry the ball and throw them off balance. It made a powerful combination. Excitement over the football team continued to spread.

CHAPTER 2

INDECISION

The following Tuesday night Bill Riley came to Fairview to speak. Danny and Kay and several others in the church invited him to stay with them while he was in town, but Tom had already gone to the pastor and made arrangements for Bill to stay with him and his parents.

Bill arrived shortly after noon and drove directly to the Channing home. Tom had football practice that evening after school, so he was unable to be there when Bill arrived. However, he hurried home as soon as football practice was over and talked with Bill about the problems and needs in Indonesia until time for the service.

Because the rally had been well planned and advertised, the church was packed.

Bill wasn't what one would call a forceful speaker. In fact, few would even say that he was a good speaker. But his sincerity and his love for the people with whom he was working gave him a sense of urgency that seemed to catch fire with his listeners. It seemed to Tom that Bill only spoke for a few minutes, but the message was over and the speaker had everyone stand.

"I don't always do this," he said. "I've never felt that man could reach hearts for dedication and a total commitment to Christ unless the Holy Spirit has first done His Work. But this is my home church, and I know a lot of you. I am especially well acquainted with you young people." He paused and significantly looked about. "Are there those here who feel that God is speaking to their hearts? Are there those who want to make a dedication of their lives, who want to yield themselves to do whatever God calls them to do?"

He waited, looking out over the congregation.

"The important thing is not whether you prepare yourself to become a missionary. It is not whether you become a minister or go into any other type of full-time Christian service. The important thing is that you be in the center of God's will – that you be ready and willing to do whatever He calls upon you to do. If you really mean business with the Lord; if you are ready to make that sort of a commitment to Him, I invite you to make it known publicly."

The instant he finished, Tom got to his feet and marched resolutely down to the front of the church.

Robin hesitated. God was also speaking to her heart. He was calling her to make a public acknowledgment of her decision to give her life over to the Lord Jesus Christ.

She might have gone forward, but her dad seemed to sense what she was about to do and laid a hand on her shoulder. Not heavily, but enough to let her know what his wish was in the matter, as if she wasn't already aware of it. Undecided, she hesitated. And the invitation was over.

Tom was the only one who had gone forward. Robin eyed him longingly. Why couldn't she have had the courage to go up and stand beside him and let people know that she too was making a complete dedication of her life and purposes to God?

Robin had planned on going over to the Channing home with Tom that evening following the service to talk with Bill, but her dad and mother objected.

"I don't think you'd better, my dear," her dad said. "You'd better go home with us."

"I told Tom I'd go over there for a little while," she protested.

"You can some other time."

"But–."

"Go tell him that you're going home with us," he insisted. "We'll wait for you."

Tom was very disappointed when she told him.

"You wouldn't have to stay very late," he said. "I'll take you home anytime you have to go."

She shook her head.

"I'd like to come over for a while this evening, Tom, but Daddy says I can't this time."

"I've been counting on having you talk with Bill,"

Tom continued. "He's a great guy, Robin. He can tell you anything you want to know about missions. And just listening to him makes me so excited to get out and get to work for the Lord that I can hardly wait."

She breathed deeply and a strange, wistful look came into her face.

"Some other time, Tom. I'm terribly sorry." With that she left him and went over where her parents were waiting for her.

"Are you ready now?"

"I guess so." Her disappointment was apparent in her voice.

They were almost home before Mrs. Evans spoke again.

"I'm sure it's wonderful for Bill Riley to be on the mission field and all that, but I can't help feeling very sorry for his mother."

"But he said tonight that his mother had encouraged him to go," Robin countered. "He said that, even when he was still in high school and told her he felt called to full-time Christian service, she encouraged him."

"I know," Mrs. Evans said, "but Mrs. Riley is such a quiet little thing and so good and kind that she'd hide her true feelings from him if she thought he wanted to go out as a missionary." She paused momentarily. "But, if you ask me, it doesn't seem right for Bill to be way off in Indonesia, or wherever he is, when he's needed so badly at home. Did you ever stop to think that since his father died his mother is all alone?"

"I honestly don't think Mrs. Riley feels badly about Bill being on the mission field, Mother. Not long ago, before she moved to Minot, she gave her testimony at young people's. She said that night that the happiest time of her life was the day Bill told her that God was calling him into full-time Christian service."

"That's what she says for people to hear," Richard Evans said, breaking in emphatically. "But I'd like to know what she honestly thinks. I'd like to know how she feels down deep in her heart. I'll bet she doesn't feel as happy as she tries to make people believe she does."

Robin's lips parted as though to answer him, but she stopped herself. At home her dad pulled to the curb and she and her mother got out at the front door. Mr. Evans put the car in the garage before going inside.

"It's getting colder now," he said.

Robin did not answer him. The cold outside was nothing compared to the cold that gripped her heart.

"Speaking of parents, I felt so sorry for Mrs. Channing tonight that I could have cried. He's their only child."

Mr. Evans nodded. "So did I. I was looking at his parents when Tom walked down the aisle. They were actually heartbroken."

Robin spoke up defensively.

"Tom says he thinks that his parents are getting used to the idea. His dad is considering having one of Tom's cousins come over and work in the store to see if he likes it. Mr. Channing may turn some of the responsibilities over to him if it seems that he's going to work out satisfactorily."

But Mr. Evans was unmovable.

"That may be all right," he said, "but it'll never work out. It isn't the same having someone in authority who's just working for wages in a business. You've got to have someone to look after things who's interested in the business, someone who's a member of the family." He folded and unfolded his paper self-consciously. "Tom isn't old enough yet to understand that, and I don't know whether he's considerate enough to change his mind if he did." Mr. Evans breathed deeply.

"Tom should realize what an obligation he has to his dad and what his dad can do for him." He got to his feet and turned to face his only daughter. "If Tom goes out as a missionary the way he says he's going to, he'll never have anything."

"I don't think that makes a bit of difference to Tom," Robin said loyally. "He's told me how he feels about making a lot of money. It just doesn't figure in his plans."

"Maybe not. But how can he hope to marry a girl he loves and expect her to go off into the jungle with him? How can he expect her to raise their children in a foreign country, very likely with a bunch of savages?" He shrugged his shoulders expressively. "Maybe there's something here that I don't understand, but

I can't see it. I think we have an obligation to our families and to our own people here in America. There's plenty to do for the Lord right here without going across an ocean to find souls to preach to."

Mrs. Evans smiled indulgently. "That's one of the reasons we've been so thankful for you, Robin," she said, "You–you've been so understanding in this thing. You haven't had any of those ideas like Tom has."

Robin fought for self-control.

"I think you have had real proof that your place of service is right here at home," her mother continued. "Look at the way you were able to lead Peggy to the Lord Jesus and the things you've been able to do in Sunday school and young people's. Why, I've had any number of mothers tell me what an influence for the Lord you have been on their daughters. As far as I'm concerned, that shows that your ministry is right here at home."

Her dad nodded his agreement.

"That's exactly the way I feel. And, speaking of Peggy," he continued, "why don't you have her over again soon? I'm sure that she is longing for Christian fellowship."

Robin smiled weakly at him but said nothing. For some reason, their arguments all seemed so plausible. Yet–.

"I'll try to do that," she promised.

After a time, she told them good-night and went up to her room. At church her parents had told her she had to come home with them as though they wanted her to study or do something else before going to bed. But once she got home, neither of them mentioned studying. They had another reason. She knew that without having them tell her. They didn't want her to spend any time with Bill if they could help it. They were afraid of the influence he might have on her.

Still greatly disturbed, she got her Bible and began to read, but the words swam before her eyes. All she could think about was the message they had heard that evening.

"Go into all the world and preach the gospel to all creation." Did that apply to her? It probably didn't, she reasoned. Not everyone was called as a missionary. Even one as dedicated as Bill Riley would admit that. Still the Lord had been speaking to her heart.

It was strange, but a few weeks ago Tom had been the one who battled with the problem of his parents and what they would say about his going into full-time Christian service. Now Tom had made a public commitment and, regardless of the cost to himself personally, he was going to follow the Lord's will for his life.

At that time Robin had been so sure that she was going to follow the Lord, regardless of where He led her. She had been so sure that her parents would understand. Now that was reversed. She was the one who was hesitating. She was the one who couldn't bring herself to go against the wishes of her parents in the matter. What should she do? Her heart cried out plaintively. What should she do?

Robin was ready to get down on her knees to pray when there was a knock on the door and her parents came in. She looked from one to the other curiously.

"Is there something wrong?" she asked uneasily.

"I wouldn't say that there is," her dad said. "Mother and I have been talking about something that we felt we wanted to discuss with you tonight."

She saw the smile playing with the corners of his mouth, and suddenly she was very excited.

"It must be something nice to cause you to come in now to tell me about it."

"We think it's nice," her mother said.

"In fact," her dad added, "we think it's something very nice." He sat down across from her. "We've been planning this for some time, Robin. It was to be your graduation gift in the spring, but you've been such a sweet, kind, dutiful daughter that we've decided not to wait. We're going to give it to you now." Mrs. Evans continued quickly.

"And you've been so sensible about this missionary thing. When I think how you could be hurting Dad and me right now, I–I can't even sleep at night."

Robin sat there quietly looking from one to the other. For a minute she fought against an almost uncontrollable desire to ask them not even to tell her about the gift, to explain that she was going to yield her life and her future to the Lord Jesus Christ. But something stopped her.

"I'll pick you up at school tomorrow noon," her

dad went on, "and you, Mother, and I will go down to the garage. You can pick out a brand new convertible.

Robin gasped.

"Dad!" she cried. "You don't mean it!"

"I've never been more serious about anything in my whole life."

"But–but a car of my own!" she continued. "I–I never dreamed that I'd ever have a car that belonged to me. I didn't think I would ever have a car I could drive whenever I pleased. I–" She threw her arms around his neck and kissed him impulsively.

"Your mother and I have another reason for getting the car for you," her dad went on. "We've been thinking that it would be a good means of helping you to witness for the Lord among the kids at school. You can take them to young people's and that sort of thing."

CHAPTER 3

FIRST STEPS DOWNWARD

Over at the Channing home an entirely different scene was being enacted. Mr. and Mrs. Channing had been sitting in the living room talking with Bill Riley. Tom excused himself after a time and went to his room to study. Still, they continued to talk with Bill, asking him questions about the people, his work, and the need in the part of the world where he was working. At last he excused himself, and the Channings were left alone.

"Bill's a fine young man, isn't he?" Mrs. Channing asked.

Her husband nodded. "He's one of the finest boys who ever came out of our church."

"Do you suppose Tom will be like him?"

"I think he can be."

"What do you mean?"

"I think it depends on the degree of dedication in his life. If he's in the center of the Lord's will, I believe we can confidently expect his life and testimony to radiate the way Bill's does."

For a long while they talked quietly. Then Mr. Channing glanced at his watch.

"Do you suppose Tom has gone to bed, Mother?" he asked quietly.

"I don't know. I think there was a light on in his room a few minutes ago." She paused. "If he's in bed, I don't think he's had time to fall asleep."

"Why don't we go in and talk to him?"

"I think that's an excellent idea," she said.

They went to Tom's room and knocked lightly on the door. Tom, who had just finished reading the Bible and was on his knees in prayer, called out, "Just a minute, please." He got up from his knees, closed his Bible, and went to the door. "I was just about ready to go to bed."

"We've been talking with Bill," his dad said. "We thought we'd like to come in and talk with you for a minute."

"Sure thing." They came into the room and sat down on the only chairs. Their son sat on the edge of the bed, looking from one to the other questioningly. "Is there something wrong?" he asked.

"There has been something wrong," his mother said, "something terribly wrong."

"But no more," his dad broke in.

The lines about Tom's eyes deepened. "What do you mean?"

"We came to tell you how sorry we are that we've tried to oppose your going to the mission field, or anywhere the Lord is calling you."

"We were thinking only of ourselves," his mother added, "and how we would miss you. All of our lives we've centered things around you and have wanted you to have the best of everything. Now that you're growing up and are almost out of high school, our hope was that you would settle near us so we could see you regularly."

Mr. Channing took a deep breath and expelled the air slowly.

"After talking with Bill," he said, "we began to understand how thankful we should be that God has blessed us the way He has by choosing you to serve Him."

Tom's face reflected the sudden joy that welled in his heart.

"You mean you aren't going to give me a bad time about going to the mission field anymore?" he asked as though he could scarcely believe what he had heard.

"Tom, we're all for it. We want you to know that we're going to try to help you in any way we can. And when you're gone, we'll be supporting you with our prayers."

Tom started to speak but choked suddenly. It was a little while before he was able to say anything at all.

"You know," he said brokenly, "I've been in here tonight, praying that God would somehow help you to see how important it is for me to follow His plan for my life. I didn't know you'd already changed your minds."

His mother's eyes filled with tears. "God has answered your prayers, son."

* * *

Over at the Evans house Robin hardly slept at all that night. And as soon as she heard her parents up, she dressed and went down to the kitchen. Her dad looked up smiling at the excitement and radiance in her face.

"Now, what gets you up so early this morning?" he asked.

Impudently she wrinkled her nose at him. "As if you didn't know." She went over and kissed him. "Tell me it's still true, Daddy. I'm afraid it's all a beautiful dream that's going to be over when I wake up.

Her mother laughed indulgently.

"It's true, all right," she said. "But I guess I found out how I rate when compared to you. I haven't had a car of my own yet, and we've been married for 20 years."

"You know you could have had a car if you had wanted it, my dear," Mr. Evans retorted.

"I know. I was just teasing you both. I'm happy that Robin is going to have a car. It will mean so much more to her now than it would ever mean to me.

Robin's eyes filled with tears. "You're the most precious parents any girl ever had."

"You're a pretty wonderful daughter," her dad told her. "This is just a little reward for being obedient and good."

She put an arm about her father's waist and squeezed him affectionately.

"I'll never do anything to make you sorry, Daddy. You can count on that."

"That's the least of my worries."

* * *

Robin wanted to tell the kids at school about the new car she was going to get, but when she got to the building, she decided against it. It would be so much more fun to wait until she got the car and let them see her in it. That would make more of an impression on them.

She smiled inwardly. She could just imagine the stir it was going to make when they saw a sleek new convertible and realized that it was her very own.

She didn't apply herself very well that morning. All she could think about was the trip to the automobile dealer's at noon. When the last class of the morning was over, Robin started for her locker. Linda and another friend stopped her.

"Why don't you go down and have lunch with us?" Linda asked.

"Oh, I'd like to, but I can't today."

"What's the matter? Have you got a date?"

"A date at noon? Don't be silly." She laughed gaily. "Daddy and Mother are coming by for me. We're going to have lunch together uptown."

"What's up?" the other girl wanted to know. "Something special?"

Robin smiled archly.

"I'll tell you all about it sometime."

Her parents were waiting for her outside. She went to the car dealer's with them, and they helped her pick out a beautiful red convertible.

"Do you like this one, honey?" her dad asked her.

Robin gasped. "Like it? It's positively the most beautiful car I've ever seen in my whole life."

Mr. Evans walked around it, looking it over with an experienced eye. "I think it's very nice myself," he told her. "I was over here a little while this morning and looked around. I told Mr. Scott I was sure this would be the car you would like."

Robin opened the car door and slid behind the wheel.

"I–I still can't believe it's true," she said. "I'm going to wake up and find out that I'm dreaming."

Her mother's smile broadened.

"If you don't think you're awake, pinch yourself."

Robin turned to her parents. Questions filled her eyes. "Then I can have it?" she asked.

Her dad shook his head.

"Not right this minute," he said. "The men will have to get it ready first. You see, it's a brand-new car that has never been driven before."

Robin tried to speak, but she could not. Tears flooded her eyes and trickled down her cheeks. She went over and kissed both her parents.

She went back to school that afternoon, but it would have been just as well if she had stayed at home. She didn't hear a thing that was said in any of her classes.

She had a car of her very own! She was the owner of a new red convertible!

Robin had a date with Tom for young people's that evening. But how could she go and sit in a meeting when she had a beautiful new car setting out at the curb just waiting to be driven? She called him up to see if he could skip the youth meeting.

"I've got something special to show you tonight, Tom," she said.

"Fine. We've got a date tonight. You can show it to me then, OK?"

"That's why I called you. I wondered if you would have any objection if we didn't go to young people's tonight."

He spoke up quickly. "Oh, I can't miss that. I've got to be there tonight."

Her voice grew icy. "We've been to every single meeting for months and months and months. I don't think it would be so terrible if we didn't go tonight."

"Well, maybe not," he said, "if you look at it that way. But in another way, it could hurt our testimonies. If we just skip out on a meeting, it's not going to look very good to the other kids we've been trying to get to attend regularly. Besides, I'm supposed to have a part in the service."

"I know all about that," she retorted irritably. "But you're only reading Scripture and leading in prayer. Surely they can find someone else for that."

"If you've got something important enough to do to miss young people's, Robin, maybe we can take a rain check on our date for tonight," he replied. "I'll give you a ring later in the week."

Sarcasm edged her voice. "If that's the way you want to be about it, all right," she said. "But I don't get a new car every day, you know."

"New car? Did you say you got a new car?"

"That's what I've been trying to tell you. I got it for an early graduation gift. It's a beautiful red convertible. I can hardly wait to show it to you."

"Sounds great."

"If you're extra nice to me, I might even let you drive it once in a while."

"That'd be OK too. I'll be keeping an eye out for you when you drive to school in it tomorrow."

She hung up frowning. That Tom Channing! Just who did he think he was anyway? If he insisted on going to young people's rather than riding in her new car, that was all right. Let him go to his old meeting.

She could find someone else to ride around with her.

That evening Robin said nothing to her mother and dad about not going to the young peoples' meeting. She left the house about the time she usually did the nights she went to the youth meeting and drove slowly down the street in the general direction of the church. Two blocks from the brick building she saw Peggy Merrill on the sidewalk and whirled over to the curb, touching the horn lightly as she did so. Peggy stared at her in wide-eyed amazement.

"Robin!" she cried approaching the new car with awe. "Who's car is it?"

Robin smiled proudly. "What would you say if I told you it was mine?"

"I'd say you were kidding me."

"It's the truth. Mother and Daddy got it for me this evening. I haven't even got ten miles on the speedometer yet."

"Where are you going?"

"For a ride. Get in."

The other girl got in and closed the door. "Oh, you lucky thing! I think it's the most beautiful car I've ever seen in my whole life."

"That's what I told Daddy when we went down to pick it out," she replied. "He was going to give it to me graduation day but decided to give it to me now, so I could get some use out of it."

Peggy squealed with delight.

"Don't you just love it to death?"

Near the church building Robin slowed.

"You were going to young peoples' tonight, weren't you?" Robin asked. There was a touch of disappointment in her voice.

Peggy noted it.

"Aren't you?"

There was a brief hesitation. "I did plan on going," Robin said, "but then I thought maybe I'd like to get a few miles on the car, seeing that I just got it and everything."

Peggy made up her mind quickly. "If you don't go, I don't think I will either."

Robin giggled. "Why don't we both play hooky? Just this once."

"I think a new car should entitle you to a little vacation. After all, you and Tom have been the most faithful members we've had all year."

They drove around for an hour or so and just before time for the drugstore to close, they parked and went in for a dish of ice cream. Word of Robin's new car spread rapidly, and the kids crowded around to ask her about it. Alex Smith and two of the football players were there. They came over to the booth where Robin and Peggy were sitting.

"Hi," Alex said.

She grinned up at him. "Hello there."

"They tell me that you've got a new car?"

"That's right. A new red convertible."

"How about a ride?"

"Anytime."

He paused momentarily. "You'd better be careful. I'm apt to take you up on that."

"Anytime you win a football game I'll give you a ride," she countered. "How's that for a fair arrangement?"

One of the guys frowned. "Just our luck. Every time we get a good thing going, we find out there's a catch to it."

Alex grinned down at her. "You don't know what you're saying, Robin. With me out there, we aren't losing any more football games. Remember?"

They sat there talking until the drugstore owner turned down the lights. Only then did Robin glance at her watch.

"Oh, I didn't realize how late it is," she said. "I've got to run."

Alex called after her. "Like Cinderella, eh?"

The taunt burned in her ears, but she didn't even let him know that she had heard him.

When Robin got home, she was half an hour later than she had told her parents that she would be. They were both sitting in the living room waiting up for her. When she came in her dad put his newspaper aside.

"Young people's must have lasted a little longer than you thought it would," he said.

She went over and kissed him on the tip of the nose. "I'm terribly sorry that I'm so late, Daddy. I just had to show off my new car a little."

"Oh, we expected that." There was a short silence. "Were there many out for young people's tonight?"

For an instant the color leaped to Robin's cheeks. "Oh, about the usual number," she said offhanded.

She went up to her room and switched on the light. For a moment or two she remained motionless. It was the first time in as long as she could remember that she had told her parents something that wasn't true. Her conscience burned within her.

She hadn't really lied to them. She hadn't said that she was at young peoples'. And she was sure that about the usual number were at the meeting. The same kids generally came week after week. But although she tried to alibi for herself, she was still disturbed. She had deceived her mother and dad as surely as though she had lied to them.

Briefly Robin debated going out and confessing to them and asking their forgiveness. But how could she do that after they had been so good to her as to get her the car? If they found out she had lied to them, they'd begin to wonder whether they had made a mistake or not.

Robin undressed thoughtfully and got into bed. Only when she was lying there in the darkness did she remember that she hadn't read her Bible that night. She started to get up but changed her mind. The next day she would read two chapters. That should make up for it.

For a time, she lay awake thinking about the way she had deceived her parents, but gradually thoughts of the new car came in to crowd out everything else. And when she went to sleep, she dreamed of the red convertible and all the boys who wanted to go with her because of it.

CHAPTER 4

DATE WITH THE STAR

The following week was the last football game of the season. Fairview had been undefeated, largely because of the ability of Alex Smith. He was easily the outstanding player of the conference, and all the girls were dying to go with him. That was one reason Robin was so excited when he stopped her in the corridor near her locker.

"You know, Robin," he said, "I was looking at that car of yours out in the parking lot this morning. It's really sharp.

"Thank you." She smiled at him warmly.

"I'm still waiting to get that ride."

"And I'm waiting to give you a ride. We had a deal – or don't you remember?"

"I remember, all right. But during the football season I haven't had much time to be thinking about dating." He grinned at her. "When that's over, you can be sure that I'll be around asking you for a date." Her heart leaped.

"I just thought I'd better give you fair warning," he went on. "So if there are any other guys hanging around, you can send them packing."

She did not answer him, but there wasn't anybody. Nobody, that was, except Tom. And he was getting to be such a prude and a bore lately that she could scarcely stand him.

"Let me know when you want a date," she said, "and I'll see if I can give you an evening."

"You'd better," he retorted. "That's all I can say. If you don't want to have a broken heart on your conscience."

Robin stared after him. She was still trembling inside. Alex Smith had asked her for a date! He had actually asked her!

Robin was so excited that Alex had asked her to go with him sometime, she felt as though she would burst if she didn't tell someone about it. Linda was leaving the school building as she came down the steps. Robin hurried to catch up with her.

"Hi, Linda," she said. "Would you like a ride home?"

"I certainly would. I've been dying to have a ride in that beautiful new car of yours."

They headed out to the parking lot, their arms loaded with books.

"I still can hardly believe that it really and truly belongs to me," Robin said. "It seemed like a dream when Daddy told me that he wanted me to go down to the garage with him and Mother and pick out a car for myself. And when we did it, I felt as though it was going to be for someone else. It wasn't going to be mine."

They got in and Robin backed expertly from the parking lot and headed toward town. For a minute or two she drove in silence. Then she glanced in Linda's direction, a faint smile playing tag with the corners of her mouth.

"I'll bet you'd never guess in a thousand years what happened to me a little while ago, Linda."

"I can't imagine."

"If you promise me that you won't tell anybody," she went on, "I'll tell you what it was."

"Cross my heart."

"Well," Robin said, "it all began a few days ago when Tom and I were in the drugstore having something to eat and I met Alex Smith."

"I see."

"And a little while ago he came up to me and told me that even though he wouldn't be able to do any dating until after the football season's over, he wants me to start going with him then."

Linda's expression did not change. For an instant it looked as though she was going to speak, but she did not.

"I don't think I've ever had anything so exciting happen to me in my whole life," Robin exclaimed. "Well, almost never."

"You aren't going with him, are you?" Linda made no attempt to hide the disapproval in her voice.

Robin bristled slightly. "And why shouldn't I go with him? Just what's wrong with him?"

"He isn't a Christian," Linda reminded her. "And you know that a Christian shouldn't date someone else who doesn't know Christ as his Savior."

There was an awkward silence.

"I don't see what that's got to do with it."

"I'm sure not the one to preach to you, Robin," Linda continued, "but I do know how wrong it is to date unsaved guys. I found out the hard way."

Robin's voice grew hard and brittle. "I suppose you're talking about the time you were going with Jack Ross."

"That's right. I thought I was going to be able to win him to Christ, but he led me away from the Lord instead. It was just the Lord who kept me from getting into all sorts of trouble."

"But you can't compare a fine, upstanding guy like Alex with a character like Jack Ross." Contempt edged Robin's voice. "He's well-mannered, a good student, and has a wonderful reputation. He doesn't drink, smoke, or swear. Jack did all three."

"But you know what the Bible says about being unequally yoked together."

Robin retorted icily, "After all, I'm not going to marry him. He just asked me for a date, and I'm going to go with him. In fact, the way I see this, it's a marvelous opportunity to win him for the Lord."

"What about Tom?" Linda asked. "I thought you were going with him."

"Tom Channing!" Robin's lips curled scornfully. "Going with him is just about as exciting as reading the dictionary. All he can think about is going to young people's and to church or what it's going to be like in Bible school or when he gets on the mission field. To tell you the truth, he's a terrible bore."

Linda said no more to her about either boy. Robin had planned on giving her a little ride. But when Linda criticized her, she changed her mind and took Linda directly home. She'd show Linda that she couldn't preach to her. After all the trouble Linda had been in, she was a fine one to give advice. Linda was jealous, that was all.

* * *

The football game with Springdale was held the following Friday night. As usual, Tom did a spectacular job as a blocking back. He threw the blocks that freed Alex for three long runs. The speedy ball carrier scored one touchdown, and the next two were long enough to set up an easy touchdown plunge over the middle by the fullback. The scoring was so swift and devastating that Springdale never did recover their composure to play the game they could. Fairview snowed them under with great ease.

The fans in the stands were yelling for Alex. But when the game was over and people were crowding around to congratulate him, he gave most of the credit to his blocking back.

"If you're going to talk to anyone about the good game he played," he said, "you'd better go over and talk to Tom Channing. He's the one who made those runs possible."

"But you were the one who carried the ball," a businessman said.

Alex laughed. "With the hole Tom opened up for me, the water boy could have made those runs. I tell you, all I had to do was follow him. There was nothing to it."

Tom grinned. It didn't make a great deal of difference to him whether people gave him credit for what he did on the football field or not. But it did make him feel good to have a guy like Alex recognize the help he was giving to the team. That meant something.

Tom dressed and went out of the locker room at about the same time Alex did. Robin was standing alone nearby. Tom went over to her.

"Hi, Robin," he said. "I didn't expect to see you here. I thought you'd be out in that new car of yours riding around by this time."

"I show up at a lot of places where I'm not expected," she informed him. She was friendly enough, but there was reserve in her voice – the warning that she wasn't too friendly with him anymore.

"I've tried to call you this week," he went on, "but I haven't been able to get you."

Robin eyed him indifferently.

"I've been busy."

"How about going to young people's with me next Monday night?" he asked. "We're having a party, you know."

She looked at him indifferently. "I'm sorry, Tom, but I may have something on Monday. I'll have to let you know later."

About that time Alex turned away from the people he had been talking to. Without a word Robin left Tom and hurried over to the new star halfback.

"Hello, Alex," she said breathlessly. "That was a tremendous game."

"We won," he replied, "just like I said we would."

"You were magnificent. I was so proud of you."

"Don't forget about the other ten guys who were out there. I had a lot of help."

"They didn't win the way they have this year when you weren't living here," she reminded him. "You just talk about the others because you're so modest. We all know who deserves the credit."

He laughed pleasantly. "I'm not going to argue with you. You know, if I had my car, I'd ask you for a date tonight. I feel a little like celebrating."

"I have my car."

"That's better yet. I've been itching to get in that snazzy convertible of yours."

Tom did not move until Robin and Alex started for the parking lot together. He shook his head. That wasn't like Robin at all. A couple of months ago she'd have flipped if anyone would have said she'd come around to the dressing room door to see if a guy – and a non-Christian at that – would take her out. What was coming over her anyway?

Alex and Robin were just entering the parking lot when Kent Gilbert saw them and came over to them.

"Hi, Alex."

"Hello there, Kent," He smiled indulgently. "How're you tonight?"

"I'm OK. You played a great game tonight. How about gettin' your autograph?"

"Sure thing." Alex took a ballpoint pen from his pocket and felt for a piece of paper. "Have you got anything I can write it on?"

Kent fished a scrap of paper from his pocket and Alex, using the fender of Robin's car, wrote his name in big letters and handed it to the younger boy.

"Thanks." Kent's eyes brightened as he looked at the autograph. "Thanks a lot."

With that he was gone.

Robin turned to Alex. "I think that was so sweet," she said. "You could have been rude to him and brushed him off, but you didn't. I was so proud of you.

"It does get a little tiresome being pestered for autographs all the time, but I guess a guy's got to expect it." He started to open the driver's door for Robin but stopped. "Robin, I–" He checked himself.

"Yes?"

"Oh, nothing."

"What were you going to ask me?"

"Skip it."

"No, you were going to ask me something. What is it?"

"Well," he began sheepishly, "I started to ask you if I could drive. Then I remembered that you haven't had the car for more than a few days and you and I haven't even had a date before. I realized that I've got a lot of nerve even thinking that you might let me drive."

Her smile was radiant. "You can drive if you want to."

He stared at her. "Do you mean it?"

"Of course I mean it." She started around the car. "Get in. I'd like to have you drive for a change."

"Say, that's great! You're a real pal." Alex got behind the wheel and started the engine. "I've always wanted to drive a car like this, but I didn't think I'd get to. This makes our family jalopy look like an old heap."

Robin smiled breathlessly.

"I suppose I'm prejudiced, but I think it's the most beautiful car in town."

"You can say that again."

They drove around town for half an hour or so when Alex drove to the highway and headed for the country.

"This is a great car, Robin," he said. "It is for a fact. But there's one more thing I'd like to find out about it."

"What's that?"

"It runs fine. We both know that. What I want to find out is this. Will it park?"

Robin felt the color drain from her cheeks, and she

was afraid that she gasped. After all, she had never parked with a boy before. That was one place where she had drawn the line. She enjoyed dating as much as any other girl, and she had gone with a good many guys. She had had a lot of good times with them, and they must have enjoyed her company. She had never lacked for boyfriends. However, she had made more than one guy bring her home early because he had insisted on parking.

Robin pulled in a long, deep breath.

She had never parked before. But then she had never gone with a guy like Alex before either. She wasn't out with just anybody.

She smiled at him, hoping that it camouflaged the wild racing of her heart.

"I'm afraid that it won't park very long, Alex," she said, trying to sound smart and sophisticated. "You see, I've got a deadline to make. If I'm not home at a certain time, I don't know what my dad would do to me."

"That's right. I remember now. You're Cinderella."

He pulled over to the side of the lonely country road and turned off the ignition.

* * *

It was after midnight when Robin finally got home. Her mother had gone to bed long before, but her dad was waiting up for her. His face was taut and unsmiling.

"Robin," he began sternly, "you're terribly late tonight."

She eyed him defensively. "I'm no later than lots of other kids my age," she retorted. "They don't have to be in so early on Friday nights."

"I don't call 11:30 early. You know that we went over all of this at the beginning of the school year and decided that you should be in on weekends before 11:30. This is the first time you've disobeyed us."

"But Daddy!" she protested. "Eleven-thirty is positively medieval. A lot of kids don't have to be in until 1:30 or 2:00, and then if there's something special they can stay out later than that. I don't know why I'm supposed to be in so early."

Richard Evans' temper flared.

"Maybe all the other kids at school can stay out as late as they want to. That doesn't mean a thing to me. I'm not responsible for them. I'm responsible for you. And I can tell you this much, young lady. If you go out at all, you're going to be in when we tell you to."

"Oh, Daddy!" Anger and disdain mingled in her voice. "Don't be so old-fashioned. Do you know what the kids call me? They call me 'Cinderella' because I have to be in so early."

His expression did not change.

"We're not going to have this again, Robin. I want you to understand that clearly."

Her eyes snapped.

"From the way you act, you must think I've committed a crime or something!"

He stood quietly, watching her as she stomped

into her room and closed the door. Then he went to his bedroom and took off his slippers and robe. Mrs. Evans stirred sleepily.

"Was that Robin I heard just now?" she asked.

"That was Robin."

There was a short silence.

"My, it must be terribly late, isn't it?"

"It is terribly late. She's never stayed out this way before." He straightened slowly. Concern lined his tired face. "I don't know what's gotten into that girl the last few days. She's never been a problem before."

CHAPTER 5

KENT'S IMPUDENCE

Robin thought she might see Alex Saturday and have a chance to ask him to go to Sunday school and church with her the following day. However, he was not at the drugstore when she went in, so she got in her car and drove around for a while. She tried to make it look as though she was just riding for the fun of it, so it wouldn't be obvious to anyone that she was looking for him. But she didn't find him anywhere. It wasn't until Monday morning that she saw him and that was in the hall at school.

"Oh, there you are, Alex," she said.

He came over to her quickly, a smile spreading across his handsome young face. "Hi. I've been looking all over for you. I was afraid maybe you'd stayed out of school to drive that sharp little car of yours."

"Oh no. Nothing like that." She eyed him breathlessly. "I've been looking for you too."

"You have? Now, isn't that something? What do you want to see me about?"

"I wanted to ask you to go to Bible club with me Thursday night."

"Bible club?" He wrinkled his nose distastefully. "Now, what's that?"

"You'd love Bible club. All the kids do."

"Maybe so, but what is it? It doesn't sound like very much to me."

"But it is," Robin countered. "We meet over at Danny and Kay Orlis', study the Bible for a while, and have loads of fun."

He thought for a moment.

"I might like to give it a try, Robin," he said slowly, "but I can never get the car on Thursday nights. That's the night Dad goes to his lodge meeting, and he wouldn't miss it for anything."

"Oh, we won't have to worry about a car," she told him. "I've got mine. And my parents are glad when I can use it to go to Bible club or something at church."

"Well, that's all right, but I don't like to be using your car all the time."

Her eyes laughed at him. 'What's the matter?" she countered. "Don't you like to drive it?"

"Like to drive it?" His voice raised. "A guy'd have to be crazy not to want to drive a car like that. It's the sharpest thing in Fairview. But I don't want you to think I just go with you because of the car."

"You let me worry about that. Will you go to Bible club with me, Alex?"

He grinned at her. "You've convinced me."

"I'll stop by the drugstore for you about 7:30. OK?"

"I'll be out in front watching for you."

Smiling to herself, Robin left him. That should show that nosy Linda Penner! She was so sure that Robin wouldn't be able to get Alex to go to church with her or be able to help him spiritually. She'd show her.

Robin knew what was wrong with Linda. She was just jealous. That was all. She probably wanted to go with Alex herself and was jealous because he hadn't asked her. So she had to give her that bit about Christians not dating non-Christians. Well, this should show her, or anyone else who got to thinking she was drifting away from the Lord just because she wanted to go out with Alex once in a while and have a little fun.

When she got home from school that evening, she told her parents about it.

"So you see," she concluded, "I am able to use the car to witness for Christ, just like you said you hoped I would do."

"I knew you'd figure out some way to use it to help you speak a word for the Lord." Her dad spoke proudly. "You're going to be my little missionary right here at home."

For some reason, his words froze within her.

Robin could scarcely wait for Thursday to come so she could take Alex to Bible club with her. That afternoon when she met him in the corridor, she was half afraid that he was going to tell her he wouldn't be able to go with her, but instead he only wanted to verify the time.

"I'm not used to having a girl pick me up," he said with a self-conscious grin. "I don't want to keep her waiting."

"You won't have to worry about keeping me waiting," she said. "The important thing is that you go over to Danny and Kay's to club with me."

"I'll be there."

She picked him up at the drugstore at the appointed time and they drove to the Orlis house together. Danny shook hands with Alex warmly, introduced him to Kay, and took his jacket into the front bedroom.

"I've never met you before, Alex," Kay said, "but Danny and I have certainly seen you on the football field. In fact, I think that everybody in town has seen you there."

Alex grinned but said nothing.

"We're so glad to have you come to Bible club tonight."

He shifted uneasily from one foot to the other. "I'm glad to be here," he said.

That night the Bible lesson dealt almost solely with salvation. Alex seemed to be very touched by what was said. He wanted to talk about it openly.

"I've never heard anything like that before, Danny," he said. "The church we go to doesn't say anything about that sort of thing. They talk a lot about peace and politics and getting rid of the slums, but I don't think I've ever heard the pastor say anything about being saved."

Danny ignored his reference to his church and the minister.

"The Bible tells us that we're all sinners," Danny went on, "and that no sinner can enter heaven. But God loved us so much that He sent His only Son to earth to die for us on the cross and be raised again. If we confess our sin and put our trust in Him, we can be saved."

Alex nodded, but it was obvious that he didn't entirely understand what Danny had said. Robin could see that he was squirming uncomfortably and looking about at the other kids. Silently she prayed for him. Danny saw his discomfort too.

"If any of you have any questions about what has been said here tonight," he said, "or if you have any personal problems that you'd like to talk over with either Kay or me, we'd be happy to talk with you. You can stay after the meeting or give us a call and come over anytime."

Alex was eyeing Danny seriously.

Just as Danny finished the lesson, Kent left his chair and came swaggering across the room to Alex.

"Hi, Alex," he said. "Are you going to show me how to do some open-field running tonight?"

Alex flushed.

"You sure showed up the rest of those sissies on the team," Kent continued. "This town ain't never seen nothin' like the way you play football."

Danny tried to catch Kent's eye, but Kent had the center of the floor, and everyone was listening to him. He reveled in it.

"Know what you've been doin' lately?" he went on. "You've been stealin' Tom's girl!"

Robin flushed crimson.

"That's right," Kent continued. "And I'll bet he's awful mad at you. It's a good thing the football season's over or he'd prob'ly let those tacklers through to smear you."

Danny spoke up quickly. "That's enough of that, Kent."

Kent turned deliberately to face him. A sneer twisted his hard young face. "You shouldn't come around this outfit, Alex. They're a bunch of squares. They'll be tryin' to get you saved if you keep on comin'."

Danny's voice rose authoritatively. "Kent," he said sternly, "I don't want to have to speak to you again. Please be quiet or leave the room."

Kent started for his bedroom, anger flushing his face. At the door he glanced back defiantly. "That's the way it always is around here," he said. "Every time I tell the truth about what goes on around here you make me go to bed."

There was a brief, embarrassed silence. For several minutes the conversation was sparse, and when it came, it lacked continuity. It wasn't long until a couple of the kids got to their feet to leave. That signaled the others to do the same. It seemed to Danny and Kay that they all left for home a little earlier than usual. When everyone was gone, Danny went out into the kitchen and sat down with his young wife.

"What do you suppose got into Kent tonight, Danny?" Kay asked. "He's never done anything quite like that before."

"He was just showing off in front of Alex. He sort of idolizes the guy because he's such a good football player. Kent doesn't want Alex to think that he has the sort of a testimony that we do."

"I felt like shaking him. He deliberately tried to embarrass Tom and Robin."

Danny got himself a drink of water.

"I don't suppose what Kent did tonight was actually much worse than the things a lot of kids his age do. They can be thoughtless and cruel if they want to be. The thing that bothers me the most is his attitude. It showed through so terribly tonight. I believe he's more belligerent than he's ever been before."

Kay nodded. "I can't help being disappointed in Bible camp. You know, we thought sending him out to camp would help him spiritually, but he certainly hasn't shown any change. If anything, I'd say that he's harder and more belligerent now than he was before he went."

"Don't blame that on the camp. All they could do was present the gospel to him. He chose to ignore it. The responsibility is his."

She wearily sat down.

"I know you're right. I guess the trouble is that I was depending too much on what camp would do for him and was disappointed when he came back no different than he was when he went."

* * *

Outside the house, Alex opened the car door for Robin and went around to the driver's side and got in. They drove several blocks before either of them spoke.

"What did you think of the Bible lesson tonight, Alex?" she asked.

He was silent for a time. 'Well, it was interesting," he said. "I'll have to admit that. And this Danny Orlis guy sure seems to know about the Bible. It was real interesting to listen to him and the discussion of the others. But I don't know that I buy this salvation bit."

Disappointment gleamed in her eyes.

"What is there about it that bothers you?" she asked, trying to sound casual. Even as she spoke, she realized that she wasn't deceiving anybody.

"There wasn't anything about it that really bothered me," he said with an indifference that showed that he couldn't care less. "I just don't think that it applies to me, that's the only thing."

"What do you mean?"

"Well," he continued, "I don't think the things I've done have been so bad. I don't drink, smoke, or swear.

And I don't run around with a tough bunch of guys." Alex paused significantly. "I suppose this salvation stuff is all right for some character who's gone off the deep end, if you know what I mean. But frankly, I don't think that I've done anything so bad I'm going to need saving."

Robin knew what she should say to him. She knew that she should quote verses that told him that everyone has sinned, that no one is righteous, that no one ever seeks righteousness. All of those things came to her mind. But how could she tell him? If she did, he might misunderstand her and get so angry he would never go with her again. And she couldn't stand that. She'd just die if that happened. She sat there praying silently for him instead of speaking out.

After a few minutes she settled luxuriously back in the car seat and closed her eyes momentarily.

"Isn't this a beautiful night?" she asked quietly.

"It certainly is." He put an arm about her and pulled her close to him. "I'm glad we have a chance to talk for a little while alone tonight. There's something I'd like to ask you, Robin."

She straightened and looked hopefully at him. "Yes?"

Some of the kids are talking about a senior class dance," he went on. "I've never gone much for things like that, but now that I'm going with you–." A grin twisted the corners of his mouth. "I'd like to get my bid in to take you to it before somebody else gets you all booked up."

Robin felt a cold numbness steal over her. Alex misunderstood her hesitation and glanced at her quickly.

"You will go with me, won't you?" he demanded.

"I'd like to, Alex," she said hesitantly, "but I–I'm afraid I can't."

His temper flared. "Now, listen, don't give me that. You haven't got a date with anyone else, have you?"

She shook her head.

"The way that Gilbert kid talked tonight I was afraid maybe Tom already had you spoken for."

"Tom and I are just good friends."

He seemed relieved.

"Then it's all settled. You're going to the dance with me."

CHAPTER 6

TROUBLE AT HOME

Robin said no more to Alex about the dance, and he didn't mention it to her. He was assuming that the matter was settled, that she had already agreed to go with him. She knew that. But she could not bring herself to tell him that she couldn't go or to explain why. There was plenty of time for that later. After all, the dance wouldn't be held for several weeks. By that time Alex would have had the opportunity to learn more about her faith in Christ and why she couldn't do certain things. He wouldn't think she was strange just because she had strong convictions.

Robin had planned on getting home before the deadline her parents had set for her that night. In fact, several times she told Alex that they would have to leave, but still he didn't start the car.

"When I'm with you, Robin," he said at last, "I can't tear myself away."

She murmured understandingly. "I feel the same way about you, Alex," she admitted, "but I've got to go now. Dad will be waiting up for me and growling like a bear when I get home now. He'll be out of his mind if I wait any longer."

Her companion sighed wearily and started the car. "If we've got to go," he said, "I suppose we've got to go. But I sure don't want to."

It was well after midnight when she pulled up to the house and went in. She paused on the porch to slip off her shoes and tiptoed in the door. But all of her extra precautions were useless. Her dad was waiting up for her in the living room. Concern had stolen the gentleness from his face and deepened the lines about his eyes. As she opened the door, he got up and went to meet her.

"Young lady, are you aware of what time it is?" he demanded.

She cringed inwardly, but when she spoke her voice was impudent and mocking. "It's 12:45."

"Do you know what time you're supposed to be in?"

She sighed her disgust. "Oh, Daddy!" she exclaimed. "Let's not go into that again!" She took a step or two toward her bedroom door as though to end the conversation, but he was not to be put aside so easily. The anger in his eyes stopped her where she was. "All you've done lately has been to harp at me. I don't know what's the matter. I can't do anything right. I get to the place where I don't even feel like trying anymore."

When her father spoke again his voice was even more stern. "You make Mother and me feel that we made a terrible mistake when we got you that car," he said. "You've been difficult to manage ever since."

Robin cringed. She and Alex had had such a beautiful evening together. Coming home to an ugly scene like this was too much. Her temper flashed. "I suppose you're going to throw that up to me again! If that's the way you feel about it, why don't you take it from me? Maybe if I had to walk everywhere I go, you'd feel better."

He looked down at her helplessly. "Robin," he said, his voice breaking, "what's wrong with you? What's happening? You've never been this way before."

"Nothing is happening to me," she retorted. "You just don't want me to have any fun anymore, that's all." Tears filled her eyes. "I used to tell the kids that I had the most understanding parents in town, but it isn't that way now. You don't even *try* to understand me anymore."

"I try," he answered, "but I certainly don't understand you. That's for sure."

She started to cry.

"Go to bed, Robin," her dad ordered. "We'll finish this talk in the morning."

He turned, stormed into his bedroom, and slammed the door.

Robin went to bed, tears streaming down her cheeks. What had happened to her parents lately? They weren't the way they used to be. Her dad had never questioned her about anything before a couple or three weeks ago. And they had almost never had words about anything. They used to want her to go out and enjoy herself the way the other kids did. Now, all they did was find fault and nag at her.

The only one who really and truly understood her any more was Alex.

By this time she had quit crying. For several minutes she lay there thinking about him – how sweet, kind, and gentle he was, how exciting it was to go with him. She didn't know what she would do if she didn't have him. There wouldn't be anyone to talk to. There wouldn't be anyone who could understand.

* * *

At the Orlis home there were problems too. Shortly after Kent had gotten into trouble with the authorities for taking part in Jack Ross' theft ring and had been paroled to Danny, he did everything exactly as he should. To be sure, he hadn't accepted Christ as his Savior, but he had given indication that he wanted to get squared away as far as the law and school were concerned. Everybody had noticed the change in him.

Now Danny and Kay spent a great deal of time discussing him and the best way to handle the situation that he was creating.

"Kent's been lying to me again, Danny," Kay said.

He pursed his lips. "I've been afraid of that. I'm going to have to have a talk with him about it. If he'll lie, he'll do other things he shouldn't, and the first thing we know he'll be in trouble again."

"I've tried to handle the matter myself," Kay said, "but he won't pay any attention to what I say. I'd just as well not even talk to him."

"I'll talk to him," Danny promised.

As soon as Kent came home Danny called him into the back bedroom and closed the door. Fright and contempt left their marks in the boy's face.

"Now, what've I done?" he blustered.

"You've been lying to Kay, for one thing."

"I have not!" His voice raised.

"You lied to her last night," Danny told him firmly. "You told her that you were going to stay at school until 4:30 and that you would be home by 5:00. You were over at the skating pond and didn't get home until 6:30."

There was a short silence.

"Well–."

"And that's only once. Kay tells me this has happened several times lately."

"Things came up," he said lamely. "I–I didn't mean to lie to her."

"Kent," Danny continued, "when you tell Kay that you are going to a certain place and are going to be home by a certain time, that's exactly what we expect. You're going to have to do it, or you'll have no privileges at all."

Kent's lower lip twisted into a snarl, and his small

face became almost ugly. "Well, get it over with," he snorted. "What's going to be the punishment this time?"

"For the next two weeks you're going to come straight home from school, and you're going to stay in when you get here. You are to be home every night without exception. You are to be home every Saturday and all day Sunday except for church services or going somewhere with us."

Kent glared at Danny. Anger kindled in his eyes.

"For cryin' out loud!" he exploded. "This place ain't like home anymore. It's like a jail!"

Danny did not soften.

"If it's like a jail, Kent, it's because you are making it that way," he said sternly. "You have to learn that you must obey us. And until you do learn that, you're going to be in trouble. You'd just as well make up your mind to do that right now."

* * *

The following day at school Alex was waiting near the lunchroom door when Robin came in. As soon as he saw her, he went over to her quickly.

"I've been looking all over for you, Robin," he said. "I was beginning to wonder whether you were here or not."

"I'm here," she retorted, fighting to keep back the tears. "But sometimes I wonder why I even bother to try to come to school or do anything to satisfy my parents."

"What's the trouble?" Understanding filled his voice.

"Oh, nothing really." She managed a weak smile. "It's just that Mother and Dad are getting impossible, that's all. I don't think anybody could live up to what they expect."

"Did they give you a bad time about last night?" he asked. "If they did, it's all my fault. I'm the one who talked you into staying out so late."

"No," she said quickly, "it wasn't your fault. I–I stayed because I wanted to." She sighed. "But I got a good going over last night and again this morning. And, what's more, they've practically put me on probation." Her lips quivered. "I don't know what's happened at our place. I can't talk to Daddy anymore. He used to listen to me and–and we'd have the best times together. But now, every time I say anything he jumps down my throat."

Alex's grin showed that he understood. "Don't get so shook up about it," he told her. "Most parents are like that, including mine."

"But they treat me like a two-year-old."

"I know. Like I said, I've got parents too. And they get just as unreasonable as yours." He paused momentarily. "It's one of those things you have to put up with until you're married."

"If that's the case," she said quickly, "I wish I were married right now."

Alex laughed. "You don't mean that."

"Oh, yes, I do. Anything'd be better than putting up with what I've been putting up with the last couple of weeks or so."

Alex followed her into line. "Is there any chance of seeing you tonight?"

Robin hesitated.

"I'd like to, Alex," she said, keeping her voice soft, "but I don't know whether I can get out of the house tonight or not."

He laughed. "Guess we'll have to be careful about how long we park after this."

The color came up into her cheeks. She started to speak but checked herself.

"I do want to see you tonight, Robin," he went on. "How about it? Don't you think you can figure some way of getting out for a little while?"

She frowned thoughtfully.

"I'll have to see what things are like when I get home. Maybe some of the storm will have blown over by the time I get there tonight."

"I *really* want to see you." His voice was insistent.

"I–I think I can manage to be down at the drugstore tonight at 7:30, but it will only be for a little while. I wouldn't even dare to drive around or anything. If I do, Daddy might even take my car away from me. He's already threatened that."

"I'll be seeing you." He winked at her expressively.

When Robin got home from school that evening, she went straight to her room and began to study. After supper she did the dishes and then went to get her coat. Her mother saw that she was getting ready to go out.

"Where are you going, Robin?" she asked.

Her dad realized what was happening and came into the kitchen. "I thought we had decided that you aren't to go out tonight."

She eyed him defensively.

"That's what you decided. I've got to go down to the library." There was a faint sneer in her voice. "I've got to get a book to read for American history tomorrow."

"Don't they have any books in the school library?" he asked suspiciously.

"Daddy," she said in ill-disguised exasperation, "you know how it is trying to get books out of the school library. All the kids from the first classes have already been in and checked them out. By the time our class gets to the library, we don't have a chance."

"It seems to me that you've got some excuse to be out every single night. Why don't you stay at home anymore, Robin?" he asked plaintively. "A few weeks ago you didn't have to be out every night of the week."

"The teachers didn't assign so much outside reading then," she retorted. The fact that she was lying to him kindled a fire that seared her heart. But she had to see Alex for a little while. She just had to. She had promised him that she would. "I can't help it if I have to study, can I? You want me to get good grades, don't you? Or don't you care anymore?"

Mrs. Evans broke in at that point.

"Now, Richard, don't you think that you're being just a little unreasonable about this? You know that we've always urged Robin to study hard and to get good grades. She's been on the honor roll for the last two years. We really shouldn't punish her by keeping her from the library when she has to go there to study."

Her husband snorted. "If she is going to the library!" he snapped.

Robin flushed. "Daddy," she said, hurt creeping into her voice, "why don't you believe me? You know you used to boast that I've never lied to you."

His gaze met hers and held there.

"A couple of months ago I wouldn't have questioned anything you said to me. You didn't give any evidence of lying, or of staying out later than you should, or doing anything that caused your mother and me real concern. But that's not true now. The way things have been going since we got you that car, I don't know what to believe."

With that he stomped into the other room and picked up the evening paper once more. For a minute or two Robin and her mother stood in the kitchen alone, staring at one another.

"I–I don't know when I've been so hurt about anything," Robin said, her lips trembling. "Why doesn't Daddy trust me anymore?"

"He's just upset because you've been out later than he thought you should be the last few times you've taken your car at night," Mrs. Evans said. "It isn't that he doesn't trust you as much as he ever did. You're still his 'little girl.' "

"I–I wouldn't tell you I was going to the library if I weren't going."

"I know you wouldn't."

"What should I do about tonight? Should I go, or should I stay home?"

"Go ahead and go, honey. I'll talk to your father about it."

CHAPTER 7

EVENING AT THE LIBRARY

Alex was at the drugstore waiting for Robin Evans when she came in.

"Hi," he said with a big grin. "I was beginning to get worried. I was afraid that you weren't going to be able to make it."

Robin sighed deeply. "So was I. In fact, I was lucky to get out. Daddy was determined I wasn't going to leave the house. If it hadn't been for mother, I'd have been stuck."

"I would've called your house about 7:45 or so, but I wasn't sure whether that would've been the right thing to do or not."

"Oh, I'm glad you didn't," she exclaimed. "That would've ruined everything."

They went back to the booth and sat down, looking across the table at each other and not talking much. A waitress came then and took their orders.

"If I were a mind reader I wouldn't have to ask," Alex said at last, "but you look worried about something, Robin."

"I am," she admitted. "I don't know what's getting to be the matter with Daddy. He–he's so unreasonable lately that I never know what's going to make him furious."

Alex smiled understandingly. "Sounds just like home. I don't even have to ask. I could tell you right now almost everything he said."

"I think I'll have him make a tape so he can play it back to me rather than get all worked up telling me the same things over and over again. Honestly, I can't say a word to him anymore but what he jumps down my throat."

"And they wonder why we don't like to stay around home any more than we have to."

The waitress came with their malts. Robin waited with what she was saying until the other girl was gone.

"I used to hear some of my friends talk about their parents and I'd feel sorry for them," she continued. "I was so glad that my dad and mother were so understanding." She stirred the malt with her straw. "But things sure have changed the past few weeks. They're both bad enough, but Daddy especially seems to want to do everything he can to make me miserable."

"Actually, my parents aren't too bad," Alex confided, "but they get all shook up about something for some reason and give me a bad time every once in a while."

He paused. "When they get too unreasonable, I just let things cool for a while and then do as I please again. That's the only way to handle them."

A horrified look gleamed in Robin's eyes. "But I want to do what my parents expect me to do. I want to be obedient and a good daughter – if they just weren't so unreasonable."

"Oh, I feel the same way," Alex went on. "If what they say makes sense to me, I do it. But there are a lot of things a guy's parents want him to do that are positively stupid." He lowered his voice. "There are times when my parents treat me as if I were a kid in grade school instead of someone practically in college. They forget that I'm grown up now."

"That sounds just like our place. The only thing that keeps me going is knowing that I won't have to put up with it forever. That, and the fact that I have you to talk to."

He grinned at her. "And I'll bet you tell that to all the guys you go with."

Her gaze met his. "Alex," she said, "please don't tease me. I'm not kidding you. This is serious to me."

"I'm sorry."

There was a brief hesitation.

"I don't know whether I've told you this or not," she went on, "but I feel that you're the only person I've ever met who really understands me."

He reached out and covered her hand with his. "I feel the same about you, Robin," he said in a hoarse whisper.

A couple of kids from school stopped and talked to them. Alex and Robin only answered their questions and got rid of them as soon as they could. When they were alone once more, Robin leaned forward.

"I've got to hurry, Alex," she said softly. "What was it that you wanted to talk to me about?"

A frown creased his forehead. "What's your hurry? Do you really have to go so soon?"

"Daddy," she said expressively, grimacing to show her displeasure. "The only way I could get out tonight was to tell him that I had to go to the library to study. I've got to put in an appearance over there or I'll really be in trouble."

Alex shrugged his shoulders indifferently.

"Just tell him that you were at the library," he said. "He'll never know the difference."

"Oh, I don't want to lie to him," she protested.

Alex laughed. "You don't want to lie to him? That's interesting."

"Well, I don't." But in spite of her denial, the color stained her cheeks.

"Don't get so shook up. I believe you."

Robin knew that she had flushed a deep crimson. She was going to stop by the library for a few minutes, just long enough so she could truthfully tell her parents that she had been there. But her conscience stabbed her. She knew in her heart that she was lying to them. She had actually left the house to meet Alex not because she had to get a library book. For a brief instant she felt as though she had to get out of the drugstore as fast as she could and go tell her parents that she had been lying to them and ask their forgiveness.

"I really have to be going, Alex," she said.

"If that's the way it is, I'd better get with it and tell you what the score is."

She leaned forward breathlessly. Strange how the very sound of Alex's voice affected her. For her, he was the most important person in the world.

"I asked you about going to the senior class dance with me," he continued, "but you didn't give me a definite answer. How about it? Will you go with me or won't you?"

She hesitated momentarily. Her gaze wavered. "I–I'd like to go with you, Alex. Honestly, I would." She spoke convincingly. "But if I did, my parents would skin me alive. I never would be able to get out of the house at night again."

"That's only if you let them find out. You can go to the dance with me and they won't have to know a thing about it."

Robin did not agree. "You don't know this town," she countered. "If I sneeze on the street, someone tells Daddy I've got a cold before I get home. I wouldn't dare go to the dance. If I did, he'd find out for sure, and I'd be in a terrible jam."

Alex raised the frosty malt to his lips and sipped it carefully. "Well," he said, "if that's the way things are, I guess I'll have to get me another date for the dance."

He eyed her obliquely. Her young body stiffened, and when she spoke, it sounded as though all the life had gone out of her.

"Oh," she said, weakly.

He measured the effect of his bombshell.

"Of course, I don't want to go with another girl," he continued. "I've never gone with anyone I've enjoyed dating the way I enjoy going with you. But you'd just as well find it out now as later. I don't intend to miss out on that dance. They say it's the biggest affair of the year other than the prom, and I'm going to be there – even if I have to take someone else."

Robin felt as though something died within her.

"It wouldn't do any good for me to go. I can't even dance!"

"We won't let a little thing like that bother us. You have dancing in gym, don't you?"

"Sometimes."

"Then you know what it's all about. I'm not worried about your not being able to dance."

"Maybe you're not worried about it," she told him, "but I am. I–I don't want to get out on the floor and make a fool of myself."

Robin's conscience stabbed at her. She should be doing something besides making excuses. She should tell him that she wouldn't go to the dance because she was a Christian and didn't feel that it was right for her to dance. She should give him her testimony and conclude by telling him that, as much as she enjoyed being with him, she couldn't go with him anymore because the Bible warns against a Christian going with someone who wasn't saved.

She could have told that to a lot of guys she would have otherwise enjoyed going with, and it wouldn't have bothered her at all. But she couldn't tell Alex. She couldn't have him thinking that she was a square, that because she belonged to Christ, she didn't do anything that was fun.

He put out his hand and took hers once more tenderly.

"I don't want you to make a fool of yourself either, Robin," he told her quietly. "I like you too much for that."

She breathed easier. She should have known that he'd be understanding. Alex was too kind and good not to be.

"I wouldn't be ashamed of you if you had four left feet and danced like an ox."

Her heart sang. Alex meant that. He actually meant it. How could she turn him down when he was so sweet and understanding. Daddy and Mother just didn't understand about such things. She wouldn't be going because she wanted to. She would be going because Alex wanted her to. What could be the harm in that?

"Tell me," he went on. "Are you going to the dance with me or aren't you?"

"I–I'll think about it."

"You do that. You do a lot of thinking about it and I know you'll decide to go with me. If you do, you'll find what you've been missing all these years."

They finished their malts, and Alex picked up the check. Robin glanced at her watch.

"It's later than I thought it was," she said, getting quickly to her feet. "I've got to be running. The library will be closing in a little while."

Alex grinned indulgently but said no more to her about going to the library just to make the lie she had told her parents become a truth.

Robin stopped by the library for the book she needed for her American history assignment but was unable to get it. It had already been checked out. Reluctantly she turned and went back to the car. Her mother was waiting for her in the kitchen when she got home.

"I'm so glad you're home early tonight, Robin," she said, lowering her voice. "Your father was furious when I intervened for you. That's all he's talked about all evening."

"I–I'm sorry." Her lips trembled. She took off her coat and scarf and sat down. "I don't know why Daddy picks on me all the time. I don't give him any reason to."

"Your daddy means well, Robin," Mrs. Evans assured her. "He's just concerned about you and wants to be sure that you will remain the sweet, lovable Christian girl you've always been, that's all."

"If this is his way of showing he's concerned about me, he's got some strange ideas," the girl said. "It looks to me as though he's more concerned with picking on me and giving me a bad time about something or other."

"Dad loves you and wants the very best in life for you," her mother said. "His trouble is that he doesn't understand you."

There was a long, painful silence. Robin wanted to tell her mother about Alex. She wanted her to know how good and sweet Alex was. She even wanted to tell her that she loved him so much her heart ached with it. But she could not put into words the feelings she was locking in her heart.

"Would you like a glass of milk before you go to bed?" her mother asked.

Milk? Robin wrinkled her nose distastefully. Why couldn't her mother treat her like a grown-up just for once? Why did she have to act as though she was still a baby? She got to her feet.

"No, thank you." Ice traced an edge on her words.

"Did you get the history book you went after at the library?"

Robin shook her head. "By the time I got there someone had already checked it out."

Mrs. Evans was instantly concerned. "What about your assignment?"

"Oh, I don't have to worry about that," she said off-handedly. As she realized what she had said, the color crept up into her cheeks. "What I mean is that I still have a study period in the morning before American history. I've still got another chance to get it at the school library during first period."

She took her coat into the living room and hung it in the hall closet. Her mother followed her.

"Robin," she began uneasily, "there's something I'd like to ask you."

"Yes?"

"You were at the library this evening, weren't you? This wasn't just an excuse to get out?"

The color drained from Robin's cheeks. "Of course I was at the library this evening, Mother," she said. Indignation crept into her voice. "That's where I told you I was going."

"That's what I told your father," Mrs. Evans went on. "But he was so upset he was going to get the car out and drive down to see where you were or if you had gone somewhere else."

Robin swallowed hard. She tried to speak but could not.

"I told him that you had never lied to us before and I was sure that you weren't going to start lying to us now."

Robin looked quickly away, not daring to let her mother see the hurt in her eyes.

The question drove its icy barbs deeply into her heart. She was deceiving her parents – deliberately deceiving them. She hadn't been that way before. She would rather have been punished than to have lied to her parents. But now she told them things that weren't true and scarcely was bothered by it.

She wouldn't have to be that way, she told herself doggedly, if they would just let her live her own life. They forced her to it by trying to hammer her into their mold. She had the right to be happy the same as they did.

Still the ache was in her heart as she went into the bedroom and got ready for bed.

CHAPTER 8

CHANGE OF MIND

The following morning Alex stopped Robin in the hall at school and spoke to her in guarded tones.

"Did you have any trouble with your dad when you got home last night?"

She shook her head. "Not this time. All was quiet and serene for a change. But I was certainly lucky. I can tell you that much. I almost got caught."

Concern leaped to his eyes. "What do you mean?"

"Daddy almost came downtown to see if I had actually gone to the library," she said. "For some reason he got suspicious and was going to check up on me. If he'd seen my car at the drugstore, he'd have come marching in and I don't know what would've happened. He probably would have made a terrible scene and I'd have died with embarrassment."

Alex snorted his indignation. "Boy, I thought *my* dad got out of line once in a while. That dad of yours must be *some character*."

Although Robin had been criticizing her father herself a moment before, she bristled slightly when Alex spoke against him.

"Oh, Daddy's all right," she said defensively. "It's just that he has some strange, old-fashioned ideas, that's all."

"You can say that again."

Robin's manner changed. "I wish you wouldn't talk that way about Daddy. You'd like him if you got to know him."

"Maybe," Alex replied without conviction. "But to be real honest with you, Robin, I don't see how I could even like him when I know how miserably he's been treating you. It makes me want to go and talk with him about it."

Tenderly she laid a hand on his arm. "Don't let it worry you," she said. "I'll be all right."

"Maybe so, but you're entitled to have a little fun once in a while."

"I think things are going to be better between Daddy and me from now on. Mother understands how things are and is trying to talk to him. I think she'll be able to bring him around."

"Somebody should."

Just outside their homeroom they paused for a moment or two before going in.

"Hey, that reminds me," Alex exclaimed, "our young people's society is having a party a week from Thursday night, and it's going to be a blast. How about going with me?"

Robin hesitated.

"What's the matter? Don't you want to go?"

"It isn't that." She spoke reluctantly. "I was thinking about Daddy again. He might not like it."

"Might not like it?" Alex echoed. "You mean he might not like it if you go to church with me? For crying out loud! How narrow can a guy get?"

Briefly Robin's temper flared.

"He just happens to feel that your church doesn't preach the gospel, Alex. That's why he wouldn't want me to go over there with you."

He stared at her incredulously. "Have you ever been over to my church?"

"N-n-no." She spoke reluctantly.

"Then how do you know what the minister preaches and what he doesn't preach?"

She had no reply.

"You should come over and see what our church is like before you start knocking it," he continued. "We're not against everything that kids our age like to do. We have some fun."

Robin hesitated, and Alex' irritation grew. 'Well, how about it?" he demanded. "Will you go to young people's, with me, or won't you?"

Her smile was weak and hesitant.

"I might be able to come," she said. "In fact, I'l make a deal with you. If you'll go to my church with me next Sunday morning, I'll go with you to your young people's party a week from Thursday night."

He smiled broadly. "Now, that's more like it. I'll go to church with you and you come to our party. Once you've been over to visit our group, I'll bet you won't want to stay in with that bunch of squares you associate with. You'll find out what fun really is."

Robin chose her words carefully. After all, she didn't want to run the risk of making Alex mad just when he'd agreed to go to church with her.

"I'm sure I'll have a lot of fun at your party," she said. "And even though I don't know any of the other kids very well, you'll be there. And that's enough for me."

His frown deepened.

"That's not what I meant."

"I think you'll be anxious to come back to our church again after you've been there once and heard the messages our pastor brings," she continued.

"Maybe I will and maybe I won't." His expression changed. "Say, what's your dad going to say if I come to the house Sunday morning to go to church with you? He's apt to get all shook up, isn't he?"

Robin shook her head.

"Daddy will be so thrilled to know that you're going to church with me that he won't know what to do. He doesn't mind my going with you, Alex. I mean, there's nothing personal in the way he feels. It's just that he thinks you're–."

Alex Smith bristled.

"He thinks I'm not good enough for you," he said. "Is that it?" His eyes flashed. "If that's the way things are, maybe I've been wasting my time going with you. Maybe we shouldn't be seeing each other anymore."

Robin gasped.

"Oh no," she said quickly. "That isn't it at all. You're trying to make something out of nothing. It isn't that he thinks you're not good enough for me. He–he just feels that–that we're not good for each other. I mean, since I've been going with you, I've stayed out later than he's wanted me to and things like that. That's what he means. He's said dozens of times that everything he's ever heard about you has been good." She laid a hand on his arm pleadingly. "It's only that he wants me to be perfect according to his ideas, and he's been so hard to please lately that he's down on anyone and everyone I've had anything to do with."

"OK." Alex laughed good-naturedly. "I'll go to church with you Sunday morning. Only you've got to promise me that I won't get waylaid and scalped when I come over after you."

"Alex," she scolded, "don't even talk that way."

"I can't help it. You've got me scared."

She ignored the taunt in his voice. "Will you be coming in time for Sunday school?"

"Now wait a minute!" he exclaimed. "Let me come to your church once and see what it's like before you try to throw the whole load at me. I'll try the morning service this time and see how it goes."

"That means I'll have to meet you on the front steps of the church. Daddy would really be upset if

I stayed home from Sunday school myself to wait at the house for you."

"OK. I'll meet you on the front steps of the church at 11:00. How's that?"

"I think you'd better make it a few minutes early," she said. "We always start promptly at eleven."

"All right." Irritation edged his voice. "I'll be there at 10:55. But don't you forget that we've got a date. You're going to our young people's party with me.

She nodded.

"And no backing out."

"I promise."

With that he winked at her and went into the classroom behind her. Robin was tingling with excitement. Alex had promised to go to church with her.

She said nothing to her parents about the fact that Alex had promised to go to church with her. For one thing, she wanted to surprise them. For another she didn't want to be questioned about how she got him to agree to go. However, they both noticed that she was in an exceptionally good mood on Sunday morning.

"Have you seen how happy Robin is this morning, Richard?" Mrs. Evans asked when the two of them were alone together.

"Yes," he replied. "She acts like the old Robin we used to have around here before that Smith kid came along."

Mrs. Evans frowned her displeasure.

"Richard, was that fair? You've never even met the boy. How can you be so sure he's all you say he is?"

Mr. Evans put aside the Sunday school quarterly.

"All I know," he replied, "is that before Alex Smith appeared on the scene Robin was obedient, respectful, and good-natured. She had the best Christian testimony of any of the kids her age."

"Robin isn't so bad," her mother defended. "She's a bit strong-willed, I'll have to admit, but I've heard you say many times that a person who didn't have a mind of her own wasn't worth very much."

"Being independent is one thing; being stubborn and resentful is something else. And that's what we've got on our hands. I don't even think we can trust her word anymore."

"Richard! Don't say that. Robin is a good Christian girl."

His manner softened. "I didn't say she wasn't a Christian, my dear. But I'm not satisfied to have her like so many of the other kids her age. I want to see her walk closely with the Lord. That's why I'm longing for the day when she'll break up with this Smith character."

Robin came in just then, and he changed the subject abruptly. She sat down on a stool near him and waited until the conversation lagged.

"Daddy," she said, "I have something to tell you."

"Now what?" He smiled at her. "Do you need a new dress, or is it something for the car?"

"It isn't anything like that," she answered. "I just wanted to tell you that I have a date for church this morning. And you'll never guess who's taking me."

Her father made no attempt to hide his pleasure. "Could it be Tom Channing?"

She wrinkled her nose distastefully.

"That creep?"

"He's a fine Christian boy."

"I know that," she went on. "But I don't like him anymore. I–I thought you'd be happy to know that Alex Smith is going to come over to our church this morning."

Mr. Evans could scarcely believe it.

"You mean he's taking you to church?" he asked incredulously.

"I've been trying to tell you that he isn't the kind of boy you think he is. He's really very interested in spiritual things."

* * *

After church that morning Alex went with Robin to meet her parents.

"I'm so glad to meet you," Mrs. Evans said. "Robin has been telling us so much about you."

"I hope it's been good."

"It wouldn't be anything else." There was a brief pause. "Would you like to come and have dinner with us?"

Alex was obviously pleased. "I think Mom is expecting me home, but I suppose I could call her."

He went home with them for dinner and, while Robin helped her mother in the kitchen, he talked with Richard Evans about school, the football team, and the college he hoped to attend when he graduated. Gleefully, Robin watched her dad during dinner. He seemed to like Alex in spite of all the bad things he had said about him. He actually liked him!

When Alex was gone and the family was finally alone, Robin turned to her dad. "Well, now that you've met Alex, what do you think of him? Is he as bad as you thought he was?"

Mr. Evans pursed his lips thoughtfully.

"I was just sitting here thinking about him, Robin. He seems like a nice boy. A very nice boy. In fact, from what I saw of him here today, I may have misjudged him."

She could scarcely believe what she was hearing. A smile broke across her face.

"That's what I've been trying to tell you," she said. "I knew you'd like Alex as much as I do, if you'd just let yourself get to know him."

Her dad frowned. "Of course, Robin, that doesn't mean that I've changed my mind about some of the things you've been doing these past few weeks. I'm still very disturbed by your attitude, by the late hours you've kept, and so on."

"I've been talking with Alex about that, Daddy," she said seriously. "We've decided that we're going to be different than we have been. Now that you approve of him, I know he's going to want to do everything he can to make you like him better than you do now."

Mr. Evans put his arm about his daughter and squeezed her affectionately. "Now you sound more like the old Robin we used to have around here."

"That's because you're different to me, Daddy. You–you make me feel as though I'm a member of the family again."

For a brief moment neither of them spoke. At last Mr. Evans stepped back and tugged at the lobe of his ear.

"I hate to bring this up right now, Robin," he said, "when we're having our first understanding in weeks, but there is another objection that I have to Alex, and I think you know what it is."

She nodded.

"You're concerned because he doesn't know Christ as his Savior," she said, "and so am I. But he is interested in Christian things, Daddy. He went to church with me today and said that he really enjoyed it. I feel confident that I'm going to be able to win him for Christ."

"That would be fine, Robin. We'll be praying for you as you deal with him, and we'll be praying for Alex too. If he were only a Christian, no one could ask for more in a young man."

She started away but came back and kissed him impulsively.

* * *

Robin Evans could scarcely wait until she saw Alex to tell him what had happened.

"And Daddy said that he liked you better than any guy I've ever brought home," she concluded.

Alex grinned. "You were right about one thing, Robin, once I met your dad, I did like him. He's really not such a bad guy."

Tears flooded her eyes.

"You don't know how happy it makes me to have you and Daddy on friendly terms with one another. I–I feel so good I could cry."

"Now, wait a minute.' Clumsily he patted her on the shoulder. "That's no way to show me how happy you are."

She dabbed at her eyes.

"I–I can't help it. I've been so worried and mixed up about you and Daddy. I–I've been praying and praying that you two would get to be friends." There was a short pause. "And now you are."

"Yep," Alex said. "Everything's turning out OK. Now, if you'll just go to that dance with me, every-thing will be great."

CHAPTER 9

ROBIN'S FIRST DANCE

Everything was different for Robin the first of the following week. She was happy and cheerful around the house, did her share of the work without a word of complaint, and studied as hard and thoroughly as she had the year before. Mr. and Mrs. Evans watched her with growing satisfaction. "You know, Richard," her mother said, "we've been so terribly concerned about Robin lately that we haven't even been able to think of anything else. But I believe we've been forgetting that she's really a very good Christian girl."

"She certainly has been different around home since I told her that I liked this new boyfriend of hers, I'll have to say that."

"Well, I can understand her reaction." Mrs. Evans sat down and lowered her voice. "She wants us to like her friends, especially one who seems to mean as much to her as Alex does. She has a real crush on him."

"He is a nice boy, Gladys," he said. "He was respectful and well mannered. In fact, he impressed me more than some of the other boys who have come to take Robin out. Even some of the Christian guys."

"I felt the same way. He was a real gentleman."

"Robin says that he's a good student too. He was on the honor roll when he lived in Minot, and she thinks he'll be on the honor roll here too."

"We can certainly be glad she picked such a fine young man. But then, she always has had good taste when it came to boys."

There was a brief hesitation. Mr. Evans' smile faded, and his face grew serious. "Of course," he said, "we must remember that Alex isn't a Christian. As far as I'm concerned, that's the one flaw in the whole picture."

His wife smiled reassuringly. "Now, Richard," she said, "don't go to borrowing trouble. You know how changeable girls Robin's age are. By next week she'll probably be going with someone else."

"Well, I'm not going to worry about that for a while," he retorted. "We can always do something about it later, if it looks as though they're getting serious."

"I'm glad you're finally coming to the place where you realize that, Richard. I have a feeling that Robin and Alex might have broken up long before this if you hadn't been so bitterly opposed to him."

* * *

Robin Evans had not entirely forgotten her promise to go with Alex to the young people's party at his church, but she wasn't looking forward to it either. In fact, she was so indifferent he noticed it as they went out to the car one evening.

"What's the trouble, Robin?" Alex asked.

"Nothing. Nothing at all."

"You sure don't act very happy about going to my church with me." Irritation tinged his voice.

"Oh, I am," she protested.

"Your church was all right," he said. "In fact, I sort of liked going over there. But we really have a lot more fun at my church. You'll find out."

She breathed deeply. "Having fun is all right," she told him, "but the important thing is whether your church preaches that Christ died to–to save sinners and that a person must confess his sin and put his trust in the Lord Jesus Christ in order to be saved. That's the thing that makes one church different from another."

"Oh, we believe the same as you do," he said off-handedly. "We sing the same songs and everything. Only we're not as hypocritical about it as you are. Just you wait. You'll see what I mean."

Robin did not answer him, but doubt clouded her eyes.

* * *

A fairly large group of kids had gathered in the educational unit of the large stone church when Alex and Robin got there. The pianist was just sitting down at the piano and the song leader was thumbing through a hymnal.

"We'll open our party this evening by singing number 321," the song leader announced.

Alex leaned over and whispered in Robin's ear, "See, what'd I tell you? That's one of the songs we sang at your church last Sunday."

The words and music were the same, but there the similarity ended. Robin would scarcely have recognized the hymn, but the other kids sang loudly. The girl in front of her was swaying slightly to the throbbing rock 'n' roll rhythm. Robin shuddered.

The next song was a beautiful spiritual. But the way it was played and sung, it sounded like any of a hundred dance numbers.

Alex' smile widened.

"See," he said, "what'd I tell you? There's some real life in our parties. We know how to have a good time."

Robin did not answer him. She couldn't.

When the song service was over, they had a brief Scripture reading and the young peoples' president read a short prayer. Then the meeting was turned over to the church's educational director who gave a short address on developing one's personality to the fullest.

Robin looked around. The kids seemed to be listening well enough, but from the expressions on their faces she wasn't at all sure that the speaker's remarks were registering with them.

As for herself, she had a difficult time following the talk of the speaker. What he said was interesting enough, but there didn't seem to be much point to it. It wasn't the sort of message that would be given at a young peoples' meeting at her own church. She'd get Alex to go with her to the next meeting. He'd soon see the difference. That probably would help to make it easier for her to lead him to Christ.

The educational director finished then and somebody put a stack of records on the record player that was brought in.

"What are we going to do now, Alex?" Robin asked him.

His eyes were laughing. "What did you think we're going to do? We're going to dance."

"Dance? You aren't serious!"

"I've never been more serious in my life. I told you that our church was different than yours. I told you we had some life in our young peoples' parties. We always have a dance."

"At church?" she echoed incredulously.

"What's wrong with that? Our church feels that dances are OK as long as they're chaperoned. In fact, they think it's better to have church dances so that the kids won't go to the other kind."

The music started and couples began to straggle out onto the floor. Alex held out his hand. "Come on, Robin."

She held back.

"You're not going to be like that, are you?"

"But I–I don't know how to dance well enough to–to dance in public."

"We already went over that before," he countered. "This will be a good place for you to practice. Then you'll be all set for the senior class dance at school next month."

Reluctantly Robin got to her feet and followed Alex out onto the floor. She had learned a few dance steps in gym class and by watching some of the dance programs on television, but this was different. She started to dance, sure that every eye in the place was fixed upon her. The music did strike a responsive note in her being. She wasn't so clumsy dancing. She just might enjoy it.

* * *

Word that Robin had danced at the church young people's party was not long in getting back to Richard and Gladys Evans. Someone told her dad about it the next afternoon and, very disturbed, he came home with the news.

"I guess I made a terrible mistake about the Smith boy Robin's been going with," he said seriously. "He's influencing her in a way that's not good at all."

"Now, Richard," Mrs. Evans protested. "Don't blame this on Alex, or on Robin either. The fault lies with the church that would permit this sort of thing. The church had the dance. The church is the one who'll be held accountable for it."

Mr. Evans paced across the living room and back again.

"I'd like to have you answer something for me, Gladys," he said suddenly.

"Yes?"

"Tell me, do you think Robin would have gone to a dance a year ago, even if it had been held in a church? Or would she have danced if she had been tricked into going there?"

There was a brief silence.

"Probably not," Mrs. Evans replied, "but at that time Robin wasn't dating a great deal. She didn't seem to have any interest in boys."

"She was going with Tom quite a bit," he reminded her.

"Him!"

"Just the same, I always felt completely at ease when Robin was out with Tom. He's a Christian gentleman."

"I know all that." Mrs. Evans pulled in a deep breath. "A year ago, Robin wasn't making many decisions for herself."

"She was making decisions for herself, all right," he repeated. "The only difference is that then she was making them in the light of what Christ would have her to do. Now she seems to make her decisions in the light of whether they will satisfy Alex Smith or not. I don't know what kind of hold he has on her. But whatever it is, it's not good."

Mrs. Evans went over and laid a hand on his arm.

"You know how it is with young people these days," she said. "They've got to try their wings a bit. They've got to dabble in the world until they find out that it's not best for them."

"You don't see Tom Channing dabbling in the world, do you?" he asked. "He's living closer to the Lord now than he was a year ago." Mr. Evans shook his head. "I don't care what you say, I wish Robin was still going with Tom. If she was, we wouldn't be having all these problems."

"But she's not going with Tom," his wife reminded him. "She's going with Alex."

The muscles in his face tightened, and for an instant his eyes glazed. "Do you suppose Pastor Reeves would talk with Robin and try to get some sense into her head?"

"I'm sure he would, only he's away from home and will be for another three weeks, I believe."

"I'd forgotten that." There was a long silence. "Tell me honestly, Gladys. Do you suppose it would do any good if I talked with her again?"

His wife shook her head. "No, I don't. Frankly, I'd hate to have you say anything to her about it now, Richard. You've just gotten things straightened out with Robin and are back on good terms with her. I'm afraid you'd only destroy the gains you've made by trying to talk with her again."

He thought for a moment. "I don't suppose it would do any good for you to talk with her either."

"Oh no," she retorted quickly. "I don't think Robin would listen to me either."

"We could wait until the pastor comes back, but I don't like to let it go that long. What about Danny and Kay Orlis?"

"They would be perfect! They've been working so closely with Pastor Reeves in the youth work at church, and they've been having Bible club in their home every week, so Robin knows them and should have confidence in them. They should know how to go about talking to her."

"That's what I was thinking," Mr. Evans went on. "Robin has respect for Danny and Kay. I think she will listen to them as well as she would listen to the pastor."

He went to the phone and called. Somehow the urgency was apparent in his voice, for Danny and Kay were there in half an hour. Mr. Evans invited them in and had them be seated.

"I suppose you've been hearing things about Robin," he began abruptly. His hands were working nervously.

"No," Danny countered, "I can't say that we've heard too much about her, but I must admit that we've both been quite concerned about her these past few weeks."

Her dad nodded. "There was a time when Robin was a real spiritual leader among the young people – or at least we thought she was. But we can't say that about her anymore."

Mrs. Evans broke in quickly. "We can't understand what's happened to her. A year ago she was reading her Bible and having personal devotions every day. She was very much concerned about the spiritual condition of the kids around her and was praying for them and witnessing to them when she had the opportunity."

"Let's see, she was the one who led Peggy Merrill to Christ, wasn't she?" Kay asked.

"That's right. And she used to meet with Peggy for Bible study once a week just to help her get grounded in her Christian faith. But to be completely honest about it, I don't think she's met with Peggy for a couple of months, at the very least."

Mr. Evans spoke up. "I think it's that boy she's going with. She's been hard to manage ever since she started dating him."

"Now, Richard," his wife said, "I hardly think that's fair to Alex. If it weren't for the fact that he isn't a Christian, we would both be very happy to have her go with him. You said yourself that he's a nice boy."

Mr. Evans took a deep breath. "It doesn't do any good for us to air our views on Alex before Danny and Kay. Right now, the biggest concern we have is what can we do about Robin?"

Mrs. Evans learned forward. "Yes, Danny, we're both about out of our minds with concern. We don't want our daughter to go off into the world like so many other youngsters we know about have done. What would cause her to be the way she is now?"

Danny cleared his throat and looked from one to the other.

"It's hard for us to believe that Robin has changed as rapidly as she has," he began. It was only a couple of months or so ago that she came over to the house one evening and talked with us for a long time about the mission field. She seemed to feel that God wanted her as a foreign missionary."

Mr. and Mrs. Evans both stiffened.

"We've gone into that with Robin." Her dad's voice was ice. "She has decided to work for Christ right here at home."

CHAPTER 10

KAY'S COUNSEL

Danny and Kay Orlis sat quietly in the Evans' living room. Danny moistened his lips with the tip of his tongue, but it was Mrs. Evans who finally broke the strained silence.

"Yes," she said, "Robin has decided to work for the Lord right here in Fairview, and we're both so thrilled about it. We can scarcely wait until she graduates so she can go on to Bible school."

Danny only nodded.

Mr. Evans squirmed uncomfortably. "Of course," he said, "there's this little problem that has come up with Robin the past few weeks that has caused us a great deal of concern. We're hoping to get it solved and to get Robin back into a right relationship with the Lord again."

"That's why we asked you to come over. We would like to have you pray for her." Mrs. Evans breathed deeply. "That is, if you think of Robin when you go to prayer."

"Of course, we'll be praying for her," Danny said.

"To tell you the truth, we've already been praying for her," Kay put in. "We pray regularly for all the kids in Bible club."

Mr. and Mrs. Evans smiled their gratitude.

"We appreciate that more than you'll ever know." However, Danny and Kay noticed that there was still something on the minds of their hosts. After a long, awkward silence, Robin's mother continued.

"There's something else that Richard and I have talked about asking you to do for us. It's really something that we should talk with the pastor about, but he's out of town and won't be back for three weeks."

"I see."

"And," she went on, "we don't feel that this matter can wait that long."

"What Gladys is trying to say is that we wonder if you would talk with Robin about the careless way she's been living the past few weeks and see if you can get her back to living for the Lord the way she was a year ago."

"We'll certainly do anything we can to help Robin," Danny assured them. "We think a great deal of her."

"And she thinks a lot of you and Kay too," Mr. Evans said. "That's why we thought it would be so good if you would talk with her."

"We'd be glad to," Danny went on. "Perhaps it would be better if Kay talked with her alone, however. She might feel more like confiding in Kay than she would in me."

"Whatever you think is best," the distraught father said.

Kay thought about it momentarily. "I've always had a good relationship with Robin. I really believe it would be best for me to talk with her alone."

"Oh, thank you, Kay." There were tears in Mrs. Evans' eyes. "Thank you so much. If you're able to help Robin, we'll never be able to repay you."

* * *

Kay wanted to invite Robin over to her home to talk with her, but things didn't work out that way. She called the Evans' home several times, but Robin was either gone or had something else planned.

Kay mentioned it to Danny.

"I think it must be that new boyfriend of hers who's taking up all her time," she said. "I can't seem to find an evening when she isn't busy."

"Well, she'll be at Bible club Thursday night," Danny reminded her. "Maybe you could see her then."

"It would be a lot easier if I could get her over here some evening when she and I could be sure of being alone," Kay continued. "But perhaps it'll work out."

During the next few days Kay tried again on several occasions to get in touch with Robin.

"I'm sorry, Kay," Robin said, "'but I just can't see you tonight. I've had a date for ages and ages."

"How about tomorrow night?"

There was a brief hesitation.

"I would like to come over tomorrow night." She spoke slowly. "I'll have to see what my homework is, though. I'll tell you what. If it works out so I can come, I'll give you a ring."

"That will be fine. I'll expect to hear from you." Kay slowly put her phone down.

"Did you get hold of her this time?" Danny called from the other room.

She went in to where he was sitting. "I got her, all right."

"When are you going to see her?"

"She said she might be able to come over tomorrow night," Kay answered, "but, frankly, I have my doubts that she will. She sounded to me as though she was trying to get rid of me as painlessly as possible."

Nevertheless, before Danny and Kay went to bed that night, they had a long session of prayer for Robin.

Robin did not get in touch with Kay the next day, but she did come to Bible club on Thursday night. She came in just before the lesson started and sat in a corner near the door. Every time Kay would look in her direction she glanced away. When the meeting was dismissed she would have hurried out, but Kay got to her before she could reach the door.

"I'm so glad you were able to come this evening, Robin," she said warmly.

"I–I'm glad I could come too." There was a moment's hesitation. "I–I'm sorry I wasn't able to come over

Tuesday night, but you should have seen the pile of homework I had to do. I was positively snowed."

"I remember how that used to be," Kay said. "There were times during my last year in high school when I was almost afraid to take time from my homework to eat."

"I really should have stayed home tonight and studied too," Robin went on, glancing uneasily in the direction of the door. "We're supposed to have a test tomorrow in English and I'm petrified about it. Daddy's been screaming so much about my grades that I–I'll just die if I don't do well on this one."

"I'm sure you'll do all right. You always have."

Doubt gleamed in Robin's eyes. Her lips parted as though she was about to speak, but she did not.

"Robin," Kay said softly, putting a hand on her shoulder, "could I talk with you a few minutes."

Color crept up into the girl's cheeks. "I–I've got a lot of homework to do."

"This will only take a few minutes."

The muscles in the corners of the girl's mouth tightened. "Has my mother been talking to you?"

Kay ignored the question. "It won't take long," she said.

"I–I'd like to," Robin said reluctantly, "but I–I've got so many studies to do tonight. If I'd known I was going to get home late, I don't think I would have come."

"We'll hurry," Kay assured her.

With that she guided Robin into the kitchen.

"Won't you sit down, my dear?" She closed the door and came back to the place where Robin was still standing motionless.

"I–I–." Her voice faltered. "What is it that you want to talk with me about?"

"Let's sit down." Once they were across the table from each other Kay learned forward smiling her friendliness. You know that Danny and I are as concerned about you kids in Bible club as though you were our own."

"Now what have I done?" Robin demanded.

"Nothing really bad," Kay said, "except that anything we do that isn't right is sin. Frankly, we've been a little disturbed about you lately."

"About me?" She bristled slightly. "I don't see why you've been so concerned about me. I'm no different than I've always been."

Kay's lips pursed as she continued, "You don't seem to have the interest in spiritual things that you had a few months ago, Robin. I suppose that's the first thing that Danny and I noticed."

"But I do," she protested. "I'm just as interested as I've ever been." She breathed deeply. "It's my mother and dad. All they ever do is find fault with me. I don't know what's been the matter with them the last few weeks. They used to be so understanding. Now I don't think they would be happy if I spent twenty-four hours a day in church."

Kay spoke deliberately. "Tell me, have you been as

regular in attendance at church and Sunday school and young peoples' as you used to be?"

The question was spoken mildly enough, but Robin winced as though it had been barbed. "Well–well–." She swallowed against the lump in her throat. "There are a lot more things that seniors have to do than juniors. I haven't had time for everything, and all the other kids in the senior class are in the same fix I'm in. And to top it off, our studies are so much harder this year than they've ever been before."

There was a brief pause.

"But, even if I haven't been to all the church meetings, I'm living as close to the Lord as I ever have. And that's the most important thing."

"That is indeed," Kay answered quietly. She picked up a napkin and folded it with care. "Do you read your Bible and pray regularly?"

Robin replied quickly. "Oh yes, I do. That's one thing I'm careful about."

The muscles in the corners of Kay's eyes tightened, but her expression did not change.

"What about today?" she persisted. "Did you have your devotions this morning?"

Momentarily that stopped Robin. A peculiar look gleamed in her eyes and the arc about her mouth whitened.

"I–I didn't have time this morning," she said, her voice faltering. For an instant her gaze met Kay's before she looked away. "I–I figured on doing my

Bible reading tonight after I get home." Her voice rose accusingly. "That is, if I don't have to stay up half the night studying just to please Daddy."

But Kay did not stop there. She continued to probe gently. "Robin," she went on, "did you read your Bible and pray yesterday morning?"

The crimson in the girl's cheeks deepened and tears trembled beneath her eyelashes. She was not able to speak immediately.

"I–I–." The words seemed to choke in her throat.

"These things are signs of spiritual coldness, Robin. Your poor church attendance and lack of regular Bible reading are the reasons we see this spiritual coldness I told you that Danny and I had observed in your life."

"Mother and Daddy have been picking on everything I've done or said for the last two months," she blurted. "I used to try to please them, but it doesn't do any good, so I just quit. I hope you and Danny aren't going to start that too."

"We don't want to pick on you, Robin," Kay told her. "That isn't the reason I asked you to come out here to talk with me tonight. I did it because Danny and I both love you and want you to have God's best for your life." The silence was long and painful. At last Kay continued. "The easiest thing for me to have done would have been to simply say nothing to you, but you mean too much to us for that."

Robin relaxed slightly.

"I–I'm sorry I lost my temper. I–I didn't mean to, but the way things have been at home lately I–." Once more tears flooded her eyes.

"Danny and I have done a great deal of praying for you and discussing you lately, Robin," Kay went on. "I don't mean to hurt you by saying this, but we can't help wondering if this boy you're going with is actually good for you."

Robin bristled. "And just what do you mean by that?"

"I understand that he isn't a Christian for one thing," Kay said. "And you know what the Bible says about believers dating unbelievers."

Robin leaped to her feet.

"I might have known you'd get around to talking to me about Alex before you got through. Well, I'll have you know that Alex is a lot more of a gentleman than some of the boys from the church I've gone with. And if you think you're going to get me to give him up, you're wasting your time."

She started for the door.

"I'm sorry if I have offended you, Robin," Kay said helplessly.

At the door Robin stopped and turned to face Kay.

"You can tell Daddy for me," she said icily, "that his little scheme didn't work! I'm going with Alex and I'm going to keep right on going with him just as long as he wants me to!"

CHAPTER 11

ROOT OF THE PROBLEM

When Robin was gone Danny came out of the bedroom, eyeing his young wife.

"I take it that your talk with Robin didn't go quite the way you wanted it to," he said.

Concern lined her face. "I'm afraid I muddled it badly, Danny. She was on the defensive from the very beginning, and I wasn't able to get through to her. I couldn't get through at all."

"It's rough trying to talk with someone who doesn't want you to talk to her," he said. With that he went to the refrigerator, poured himself a glass of milk, and came back to sit down. "Richard and Gladys aren't going to be very happy when they find out what took place. Did you get to talk to her about dating Alex Smith?"

"Did I?" Kay echoed. "That's what sent her storming out of here. She was halfway listening to me until

I said something about him. That ended the conversation as far as Robin was concerned."

Danny frowned thoughtfully. "I don't suppose it makes any real difference whether she gets mad or not. If she feels that way about him, nothing you could have said would have changed her mind."

"I've never tried to talk with anyone who was as determined to have her own way as Robin is," Kay said. "I was concerned about her before, but I'm more concerned than ever about her now. She's so wrapped up in Alex that she can't think straight when it comes to him." She toyed with the design on the tablecloth. "Danny, what can we do about her?"

He shook his head.

"I don't know whether there's anything we can do except to pray. If a person has an open mind, he can be persuaded that he's wrong, but Robin probably would never admit that there's anything wrong with her relationship with Alex."

"I'm sure she wouldn't." Kay paused. "Robin isn't at all the same girl who used to come to Bible club and take such an active interest in the things of the Lord. She's arrogant and defiant and secretive – even belligerent."

"That's just about what Richard and Gladys told us we could expect."

"I know." She spoke slowly. "But I tried to make myself believe there was some mistake."

"I think we need to remember that this sort of thing can happen to any of us," Danny said, "regardless of how close or how long we have been walking with the Lord. We've got to recognize that and to be alert to the danger signals that will tell us when we're drifting from God."

"I know that," Kay continued. "But I'm still bothered by what's happening. Of all the kids in Bible club, Robin is the last one I would have suspected would go this way."

"That's just what I mean."

Kay was silent for a minute or two.

"I suppose going with an unsaved guy could have this sort of an effect on a girl," she said, "even though the boy is a good student and a clean young man, morally."

"I'm sure Alex is part of the trouble," Danny said thoughtfully, "but I've been sitting here trying to figure this out since we've been talking. I think the real trouble is something else that's even more important."

"Like what?" Kay wanted to know.

"It hasn't been so long ago that Robin felt called to full-time Christian service," he said. "You remember the time she came over and talked with us about it, don't you?"

Kay nodded. "Of course. She was concerned about what her parents would say when she told them."

"Exactly. And her parents did object when she informed them she was going to prepare herself as a full-time servant of the Lord and would probably be going somewhere abroad as a missionary."

Kay frowned. "I'd never thought of that before, Danny, but what you say is true. Her mother told me herself that she thought it was the most ridiculous thing she had ever heard of and that she and Richard were trying to talk some sense into Robin's head."

"They talked some sense into her, all right. And I think they got her that car to seal the bargain. I wonder if her spiritual downfall didn't begin the moment she gave in to their demands and turned her back on God's call?"

For a long while Kay considered Danny's question.

"That makes it seem altogether different, doesn't it?" Kay asked at last. "Robin told me herself that she had never asked for a car or even thought about getting one of her own until her parents told her they were going to get it for her." She breathed deeply. "Poor Robin!"

"Poor parents!" Danny echoed. "Think of the blessings they're missing right now by denying her to the Lord's service. Think of the agony they'll have when they finally discover that what is happening to Robin is directly the result of their refusal to allow her to serve the Lord."

"Are you going to say anything to Richard about it?"

He nodded.

"I'll talk to him when I see him tomorrow, but I doubt that it'll do any good. He's set in his ways too."

"I'm wondering myself if it'll do any good," Kay said, "but for a different reason. Robin doesn't act to me as though she's the slightest bit interested in preparing for any kind of Christian service. Right now, she's tasting the fruit of the world and seems to be finding it so good she's determined to keep her back turned against God."

* * *

Robin stormed out of the Orlis home and out to her car. Kay Orlis didn't need to think she could talk to her that way! She was just as good a Christian as Kay or Danny or anyone else in that stupid old Bible club. The trouble was that Kay thought anything that was fun to do was wrong. It was no wonder she couldn't get Alex interested in coming to Bible club or in going to church with her. The people in her church were a bunch of fanatics, and he was smart enough to see it.

Angrily she slammed the car into gear and took off, peeling rubber. She had driven two blocks at a furious pace before she came to her senses and let up on the accelerator.

As she did so it seemed that a portion of her anger left her. She really shouldn't blame Kay and Danny. Her parents had undoubtedly gotten hold of them and asked them to talk with her and try to get her to break up with Alex. Well, it wasn't going to work.

When she got home and put the car in the garage, she saw her dad standing before the living room window. Mentally she braced herself and went inside.

"Well, how was Bible club?" he asked.

"All right." Her voice was frigid.

"You're home a little later than usual, aren't you?"

She whirled to glare at him. "If you want to know why I'm late, ask Kay Orlis. She cornered me tonight after club and gave me the third degree. So, if you don't believe what I tell you, you can call her up and ask her."

"I didn't say that I didn't believe you, Robin," he told her almost plaintively. "I just asked you a question."

"Yes, but I know what you meant by it. You were cross examining me the way you always do when I come home at night."

He started to reply hotly but stopped himself.

"And for your information, Daddy," she continued, "having Kay talk with me about giving up Alex didn't work. I don't care what you do, you're never going to break us up!"

She stomped into her bedroom and slammed the door behind her. Her dad would pick up his phone now and talk to Kay, she told herself. He'd have to find out what happened. Well, let him call her! She wasn't going to be shoved around by Kay and Danny, or her parents, or anyone else. They'd just as well quit trying.

She was still angry as she undressed for bed.

She could understand her parents getting worked up about Alex. They didn't understand her and couldn't stand the idea of her having any fun. But Kay was different. She had always thought of Kay as one of her best friends – a person she could go to about almost anything and feel sure that she would understand.

Kay and Danny had it in for Alex the same way her parents did. That must be it. Just because Alex didn't go to their church and Sunday school and testify every time someone asked for testimonies, Kay probably thought that Alex was a bad influence on her. Well, he was just as nice as a lot of Christian guys. In fact, he was a whole lot better than some of them.

She sat down on the side of her bed and fingered her Bible thoughtfully.

Besides, she just knew that Alex would accept Christ as his Savior one of these days. In a way she felt that he must believe now. He'd almost have to be a Christian to be so nice and kind and good. He didn't understand very well because his church didn't teach the Word as plainly as it should, but he had gone along as far as his church had taken him. And besides, she loved him so very, very much.

That night Robin spent a long time reading her Bible and praying. She would show Kay Orlis. She'd show her and her parents and everyone who knew her that she wasn't any different than she had ever been. She was going to live for the Lord in a way that she had never done before.

But even as she made such a promise to herself, a dull aching welled in her heart. She wanted to live for the Lord and keep Alex too. Whatever happened, she couldn't let him go. And yet, she knew she couldn't live the way God wanted her to live unless she did give up Alex and prepare herself for full-time Christian service.

That was something that even her parents didn't want, concerned as they were about her. A strange, crooked smile came to her face. What would her dad say if she told him that she was either going to go with Alex or go out to Africa or some other place halfway around the world as a foreign missionary? That would make him think!

In the other room Richard Evans dropped in anguish to his knees, praying for his daughter. Even as he did so, he knew that her rebellion was far from over. Yet a fleeting assurance came to him that God had heard their prayers and would, one day, bring Robin back to Himself.

THE DANNY ORLIS SERIES

The Danny Orlis series, by Bernard Palmer, delivers a blend of adventure, mystery, and suspense through various settings—from the Canadian wilderness to Guatemalan jungles. Danny Orlis, an adept outdoorsman, skilled athlete, and committed Christian, employs his quick thinking, calm bravery, and biblical solutions to confront everyday problems and hair-raising dangers. Early stories focus on Danny navigating school life, sports, and outdoor challenges, while in later books, Danny and his wife Kay provide wisdom and guidance to youngsters facing lifelike situations and challenges. Having sold over two million copies, this series has made Palmer a renowned author in Christian youth literature. Palmer is also the author of the Felicia Cartright series and various other series for Christian youth.

AVAILABLE FROM WWW.ANEKOPRESS.COM

www.ingramcontent.com/pod-product-compliance
Lightning Source LLC
Chambersburg PA
CBHW060503300726
48975CB00008B/2617